WHERE MAGIC BEGINS

By

Faith Prince

To my wonderful parents,

for all your love and support

Chapter One

Zoeli

"Sorry, Zoe, but this isn't working out—" I shut off my phone without reading the rest of the message. There's no point. I already know what it's going to say.

I squeeze my eyes shut, tears burning in the corners, threatening to escape. I won't let them out. He's not worth it.

Yesterday, when he came over, I saw him peeking down the hallway, trying to get a glimpse of my sister. That's when I knew it was over. Even though I expected it, rejection still stings. I know why I was tossed out like yesterday's trash. Saria. Pretty, perfect, backstabbing Saria.

At least it's Friday. Outside, tendrils of sunlight peek through millions of tiny crevices between leaves and trees, as if a fairy sprinkled glitter over the forest. The racket of a revving lawn mower drowns out the song of morning birds.

Downstairs, glass shatters, and thump! *Mom.* My heart is in my throat as I sprint down the steps, two at a time. Mom lays on the kitchen floor, arms bent overhead, legs sprawled out. Shards of glass and pieces of blue ceramic are scattered everywhere. A half-eaten English muffin soaks in a puddle of orange juice.

I crouch beside her. "Mom, are you okay?"

Mom moans, her eyes half shut. Blood pours from a gash on her forehead. I grab a clean dish towel and press it against her wound.

"I'm fine." I hate when she has that stubborn tone. She's definitely *not* fine. The towel is already soaked in blood.

"I think you need stitches." How many times would this continue to happen? Which time would be the last?

"No, I'll be okay," Mom says.

"What's going on?" Dad stands beneath the kitchen archway. Grass clippings cling to his hair and t-shirt. "Alaina! What did you do? You promised me that last time would be the **last** time."

"Dad, stop. I'm sure she did what she thought was right." The truth is: I'm mad at her, too, but it isn't the right time for that conversation. First, we need to make sure Mom's okay. Then, we can rip her a new one.

"Mom? Not again!" Saria appears in the doorway, her arms folded across her lacy pajamas. She steps barefoot over the broken glass. "Get out of my way." Saria waves her arm at me, motioning for me to move. I step aside.

Saria kneels beside Mom, brushing greasy blonde strands out of her eyes. "It's too early for this crap." Blood gushes, pouring down Mom's cheeks and neck. My heart bangs against my rib cage. We really should go to the hospital.

Saria traces the wound with her thumb. Her palms make circles over the injury, golden mist swirling around her fingertips. I watch as Mom's skin knits back together. "Done." Saria wipes her hands on her thighs. She breathes heavily, sweat glistening along her hairline.

"Is everything okay?" The voice comes out of nowhere.

I jump and spin around, searching for who just spoke.

Mallory watches us, her hand on her chest. "I'm sorry," she says. "I didn't mean to startle you. The door was wide open…" She gestures to the front door. Dad must've forgotten to close it when he rushed inside to help Mom.

"I lost track of time!" Saria keeps her head down, hair covering her face. "I'll be right back. I need to get dressed." Her footsteps disappear up the stairs.

"What happened?" Mallory asks, surveying the mess.

"Oh, just a little fall," Mom laughs as Dad helps her to her feet. I open the closet and grab a broom.

"That's A LOT of blood," Mallory says. "Maybe you should go to the ER."

My heart hammers in my chest as I sweep up the broken glass. How are we going to explain this to Mallory? If we aren't careful, people will get suspicious.

"Oh, don't be silly," Mom says. "I'm fine." She's pale as a ghost, slumped against Dad's shoulder. She looks as *fine* as death warmed over.

Mallory raises her eyebrows, her brow creasing up. "Are you sure? I can call." She holds up her cell phone.

"No, that'll be okay," Dad says, helping Mom down the hallway and towards their bedroom. "She'll rest it off."

There's no chance in hell that Mom is going to the hospital now. Healing magic flows through her veins. I wonder what that looks like on a CBC. If they found out our secret, we'd all become lab rats. Well, except maybe me. My magic is so pitiful that they wouldn't waste their time.

I empty the dustpan, the broken pieces sliding into the trash. "I have to catch the bus." I sling my backpack over my shoulder.

"Zoe, do you want to ride with us?" Mallory asks.

I freeze for a moment, shocked by the invitation. Mallory is new to town. She must not know the history between Saria and I. "Thanks, but I'll be fine on the bus."

Chapter Two

Saria

I sit at my vanity, staring through puffy eyes at my reflection. My skin is marred by angry red acne. Gross. I can't believe Mallory saw me like this, even if it was for just a minute.

I open the top drawer, the items inside dinging and chiming as they clatter against each other. I don't own a hairbrush or makeup. Instead, I rummage through a plethora of crystals, sliding my fingers over them, gauging their energy. Healing Mom drained a lot of my magic. I'll need an extra powerful crystal today.

I wrap my fingers around a big chunk of clear quartz. Closing my eyes, I channel in on my energy, deep in my core. It's always there: easy to find, simmering but solid, a dense orb of light. I focus on the energy, willing it to be released. It's like turning up the fire under a burner. The energy boils, and then it melts, scorching lava flowing through my veins.

I imagine myself with flawless skin, rosy cheeks, and long curled eyelashes. Moving onto my hair, I fill in my roots, add body and shine, thick waves cascading down my back.

When I open my eyes, the quartz glows in my hand, illuminating the room with golden light. I look exactly as I had envisioned, not a hair out of place.

"You sure got ready quick."

I spin around in my seat. Mallory stands in my bedroom doorway. How long was she there? How much did she see?

"What's that?" Mallory asks, looking at my hand.

My heart races like a jackhammer. "Oh, nothing," I say, slipping the crystal back into my drawer. It's still blazing hot. Hopefully it doesn't set my furniture on fire. "Let's go." I stand up.

Mallory stares at the drawer, not moving. For a moment, I wonder if she's going to open it and demand to know what's going on. "Let's go," I repeat.

Mallory's eyes narrow, but then she smiles. "After you."

I slide into the passenger seat as Mallory climbs into the backseat. Giselle is in the driver's seat, visor down, applying her lipstick. "Finally," she says, hitting the gas. "We're going to be late."

"Don't worry." I smile. "We'll make it." As we pull up to the traffic light, it turns green.

"That's odd," Mallory says from the backseat. "It just turned red."

I shrug. "Must be good luck." Why does Mallory keep questioning me? Has she figured out my secret? Or am I just paranoid? Lately, I have this strange feeling that someone is watching me…biding their time. I shake my head. I'm losing it.

Giselle parks her Range Rover in the high school parking lot. As soon as my feet hit the pavement, Penny runs towards me. "Hi, Saria!" Penny says, grinning from ear to ear. "Your hair always looks so amazing."

Everyone is affected by my thrall to varying degrees, depending on their level of psychic resistance. Penny is pathetically weak. She follows me around like a lost puppy dog.

"It looked like crap an hour ago." Mallory smirks. On the other hand, Mallory seems immune to my powers. I glare at her, but she's unaware, already leaning in and whispering to Giselle. She tosses her hair as they both burst into laughter. Are they talking about me? I'm not used to feeling insecure around Giselle. Everything seems to have changed since Mallory moved to town.

When we were in pre-school, Giselle and I played with Barbies, jump ropes and doll houses together. When we grew older, she called me giggling after her first kiss, and then crying after her first heartbreak. Giselle wouldn't turn against me… Would she?

The world sways, and then vertigo engulfs me. I stagger, the world swirling around me, reaching for something solid to steady myself on. What's happening to me?

I don't realize I'm leaning against a car until the door opens. "Hi, Saria," Keisha says, closing her car door behind her. "Are you okay?"

The world comes back into focus. "Hey, I'm fine." I laugh nervously, wiping my sweaty palm against my knee. "I didn't eat breakfast this morning." Penny lingers nearby, her brow furrowed in concern. Giselle and Mallory are long gone.

"You better eat! We're playing the Raiders later. They're undefeated, and most of their players are twice our size." Keisha says.

"Their winning streak ends tonight. We'll destroy them. Easy." I say, my confidence returning.

"Um, hi, hi Saria." A guy fidgets with strings that dangle from his hoodie. I can't remember his name. "What are you up to this weekend? I'm, um, having a party..."

"I'm busy." I can't escape the nagging feeling that someone is watching me. The back of my neck tingles, and I rub my finger over the birthmark there: the light-brown mark that looks like a three-pointed crown. I glance over my shoulder, eyeing the bushes beyond the parking lot. As I stare, the branches sway. Are they rustling in the wind, or is someone back there? A shiver crawls up and down my spine.

"Hey, Saria." I turn and yelp as someone falls into step beside me. "I'm sorry. I didn't mean to scare you."

I press my palm against my pounding heart. I'm going insane. Logan places his hand on my shoulder, and suddenly I'm okay. "You just startled me. I've been so jumpy lately." Logan looks concerned, so I force a smile. "I'm fine."

Logan's pencil thin arms sway too fast, out of rhythm with his oversized feet. "I've been thinking about some ideas for our project. Are you free tonight? We should get started."

"Saria has softball tonight." Penny brushes an errant strand of red hair out of her eyes.

"I'm free tomorrow night," I say. "Does that work?"

"Yeah, that sounds great. See you tomorrow." Logan's hazel eyes shine behind his thick glasses. As he walks away, he looks over his shoulder once, a goofy grin still spread across his face.

Penny's mouth gapes open. "You're going to hang out with Logan on Saturday night?"

"I have to work on this project," I say.

"On a Saturday? Won't Chad be mad?" Penny asks.

"I'm sure it won't take all night," I say.

"Chad's a big boy. He'll get over it." Keisha shrugs. "And if not, bye-bye!"

As I walk through the double doors into Mountainside High School, I can't get a second to myself. Classmates surround me, complimenting me, demanding a piece of me. But what do they really want from me?

I need a moment to think, to try to figure out why I'm so on edge lately. Guys stare and fumble their words, enraptured by my thrall. Even in the midst of admirers, I feel all alone. No one knows me. The real me.

Chad waits at my locker, arms folded across his chest, biceps bulging beneath his tight t-shirt. He sweeps me into his arms, tangles his fingers into my hair, and presses his mouth against mine. "Good morning, beautiful." Chad smiles, revealing perfect white teeth.

"Good morning," I mumble, looking down.

"What's wrong?" Chad asks.

"I'm not sure," I say, looking over my shoulder. The hallway is full of people, so many faces drifting by, lockers slamming, hands slapping hi-fives. I can't shake this feeling. "I think someone is watching me," I say.

"Of course they are," Chad says. "You're beautiful." I hate when he looks at me with those glassy eyes, like he isn't even seeing *me*, only my magic. I wish I could shut it off.

"A lot of girls are," I say.

"Not like you," Chad says. "I've never seen anyone as beautiful as you before."

He's lying, but he doesn't even know it. The truth is: I'm not beautiful. Zoeli is my identical twin, but Chad isn't attracted to her. If he had been, maybe Zoeli wouldn't hate me so much.

My emotions have weight, crushing my throat. I swallow them down; their sharpness ripping into my stomach. I'm a terrible sister. If I wasn't so proud, I would admit that I made a mistake. But now, I'm in too deep. She'll never forgive me.

"I love you," Chad whispers.

The knot in the pit of my stomach tightens. If my magic was stripped away, he wouldn't love me. The truth is: I'm nothing but a big fat phony.

Chapter Three

Zoeli

I get off the school bus and scope out the scene. One security guard is looking the other way. The other is scrolling through his phone. It's the perfect opportunity. I take a sharp left and sprint past the school building, cut through the baseball field, and disappear into the woods. At the end of the dirt path, Justin leans against the side of a small wooden bridge, his arms around Yazmin. She smooths a few unruly strands of Justin's green and blue striped Mohawk.

As I come closer, Yazmin's eyes widen. "What's wrong, Zoe?" I'm the worst at hiding my emotions. I should just walk around with my fingers in the shape of an "L" on my forehead. Justin hands me his vape pen. I take a long drag.

"My mom was sick again this morning. She passed out in the kitchen."

"Oh, no! Is she okay?"

"Yeah, this time, but I worry about her. Oh, and Ryan broke up with me. Via text message."

"What a jerk!"

"He was probably just using me to try to get closer to Saria. Just like Brad and Vinny admitted after they dumped me."

"You don't need a boyfriend, Zoe. You're a strong independent woman. We don't need men!" Yazmin throws her fist in the air, and I follow suit.

"Really?" Justin raises his eyebrows.

"I don't need you, babe. I choose you. There's a difference." Yazmin pecks Justin on the cheek. "You respect my intelligence and treat me as your equal. Ryan's a shallow douchebag."

Justin nods. "I never liked that kid. I'll kick his ass."

"Me too," a male voice calls from the end of the path. Scott puffs out his puny chest as he approaches.

"There will be no fighting." Yazmin's voice has an authoritarian tone. She glares at Justin. "The principal already warned you, one more fight and you'll be expelled."

"Yaz is right. I need you guys here for my sanity. It's hard enough living everyday with Princess Perfect. Sometimes I can't believe that we're related, let alone identical," I say.

"You're identical?" Scott's jaw drops.

"Yeah, but she dyes her hair blonde."

"It's not just the hair, Zoe. I don't think you look alike." Scott howls as Yazmin kicks him in the shin.

"You can say it. She's prettier than me." Or she appears to be because of her magic. "It doesn't matter. I have more going for me than my looks." It's true. I wouldn't want to be defined by my outer beauty. Still, it sucks being the ugly sister.

I dig inside my backpack, rip a piece of paper out of my notebook, and hand it to Yazmin. "I've been working on lyrics for our new song."

Scott leans in to read over her shoulder. "Wow, this looks really good."

"I can't wait for practice tonight." Yazmin checks her watch. "I better head back. Ms. Harrison has a conniption if anyone is two seconds late." She tucks her purple-streaked hair behind her ears and grabs Justin's hand. They head down the path, Scott a few steps behind. Yazmin looks back. "You coming, Zoe?"

I shake my head. "I have study hall first period. I'm just going to hang out here for a bit." A bird flutters overhead and then lands on the branch of an old oak. It hops along the branch, brown wings flapping, chirping loudly. It reminds me of when Saria and I used to bird watch together. I swallow hard. Even after a year, the sting of betrayal is just as strong.

"You sure?" Scott asks.

"I'll be fine." I look up, but the bird's gone.

I slide my phone out of my pocket and text Dad.

Is Mom okay?

She's still sleeping. If it's anything like last time, she'll be asleep for days.

Keep an eye on her. I'm worried.

I'll watch her like a hawk.

The bushes behind me rustle. I spin around. A flash of black and then it's gone. My heart races. What was that? As I walk towards school, it feels like the trees are closing in on me. The leaves make shadows on the ground; dark shapes that remind me of teeth. The dirt trail suddenly seems a million miles long. I walk faster.

Thump. I whirl around. There's no one there. Thump. I suck in a shaky breath. I need to chill. I'm in the woods. There's all kinds of animals out here. I'm probably freaking out over a squirrel. Still, something feels wrong. I turn back around.

The boy leans against an old oak tree. He's close enough that if I reach out, I could touch him. Where did he come from? I didn't hear any footsteps. No one was there a second ago.

Dressed in all black, he watches me through the biggest and darkest eyes I've ever seen. They could suck me in like a black hole. He's tall and muscular and my intuition tells me that he's powerful. Very powerful.

In summary, he's gorgeous and terrifying all at once. Since I value my life over cheap thrills, I'm getting the hell out of here. I break out into a run. Footsteps pound behind me. "Zoeli!" The boy shouts. My blood is like icicles in my veins. He knows my name. This was not a chance encounter. "Zoeli, stop!"

"Not a chance, creep!" I speed up. He's right behind me; predator chasing prey. My pulse hammers so loud in my ears that I'm sure he can hear it.

I don't turn back around until the school is right in front of me. He's gone. Who is he? What does he want? I push the double doors open and enter the school building. Safe, for now.

Mom warned me about people who want to hurt us just for being who we are. Have they found me? I want to call her, but she's passed out.

In the hallway, Yazmin is arguing with a security guard. "Miss Hamdan, do you think that apparel is appropriate for school?"

Yazmin examines the black letters on her purple t-shirt that read "When a man gives his opinion, he's a man. When a woman gives her opinion, she's a bitch."

"It's a Bette Davis quote," Yazmin says, hands on her hips. "Women need to stand up, expose and defy these double standards. I think it's very appropriate and delivers a positive message."

The security guard sighs. "We will have to let Principal Meyers be the judge of that."

"It's just a word. Do you think that anyone in this school hasn't seen it before?"

"Yazmin, walk with me to Principal Meyers office. Now."

"Fine, I'll go, and I'll tell Principal Meyers exactly where he can put his dress code." Yazmin sees me. "Zoe, are you okay? You look like you've seen a ghost!"

I brush sweat-soaked hair from my eyes. "I'm good," I lie. "Girl power!" I cheer her on, effectively changing the subject. Yazmin flashes her bicep before she disappears into the principal's office.

Chapter Four

Saria

"Those girls look tough," Giselle says.

"We got this," I say.

The home team takes their positions on the field. I trot over to the pitcher's mound, pushing the dirt around with my cleats.

"Warm up?" Keisha's ready in her catcher's gear.

"Nah." I shake my head. I need to reserve my powers for the game.

The first batter jogs up to the plate. For a moment, I close my eyes. My power simmers just below the surface of my skin. I channel my magic, using as much force as I can muster. The energy shoots through my pitching arm, a geyser erupting at lightning speed.

I throw the first pitch. It whizzes by the batter before she even has a chance to swing. "Strike one!"

A half hour later, I've racked up three innings of shut-out pitching and four home runs. I'm single-handedly winning the game; score 7-0.

Giselle, on the other hand, isn't having a great game. After her fourth strike out, she sits in the dugout with her head down. She knocks her cleats together, stirring up a cloud of brown dust.

"It's okay," I say, patting her shoulder. "You'll blast it out of the park next time."

Giselle shakes her head. "No, I won't." She looks up, wiping the wetness beneath her eyes. "Not everyone is as perfect as you."

I'm far from perfect. If only Giselle knew the truth: she'd probably outperform me if I wasn't using my powers. I'm still thinking about what to say, how to make this better, when a voice breaks into my thoughts.

"I see you moping." Giselle's mom stands on the other side of the chain link fence. "Pull yourself together. You're embarrassing me."

Giselle jumps in her seat. "Mom? How long have you been here?"

"Long enough."

"Mom, I, I, I'm not feeling well tonight."

"Excuses are for losers."

Giselle's mom has always been tough on her, but I'm taken aback by the vitriol in her tone. "Hi, Mrs. Baron," I say, racking my brain for any way to change the subject. The last time I saw Giselle's mom she mentioned being hired for a new job. "How's your new position going?"

Mrs. Baron smooths her slick bob. "It's going well. Thank you so much for asking, Saria. But that's enough about me. Your pitching is incredible! You never cease to impress me with your talent."

I cringe. Giselle turns back around, clanging her cleats together, harder and harder, dirt spinning around her feet like a mini-tornado. Clink, clunk, clank! I cough, waving the dirt away from my face. "Giselle, what's the matter with you?" Mrs. Baron's hands are on her hips, fingers curling over her black pin-striped blazer. "It's bad enough to be a poor player. You don't have to be rude, too!"

"Hmmmph." Giselle stares at the ground.

"I apologize for my daughter's behavior, Saria. I'll deal with her when we get home. It was lovely seeing you." Mrs. Baron stalks away.

"You're up, Saria," Coach Nelson says.

"Giselle, I'm so sorry. Your mom was out of line," I say.

"It doesn't matter. I don't care what that woman says. I don't care about her at all. I don't care."

"Giselle," I start.

Giselle puts up her hand. "Stop. I don't want to talk about it."

"But, Gis—"

Giselle slams her fist against the wood bench. The dugout roof casts a dark shadow over half of her face. Her brown eyes narrow into slits. "I said stop. Now GO. You're up." Giselle's voice is as cold as her expression. Icicles slide down my spine.

I shake my head, trying to regain my composure. I need to keep my head in the game. I can talk to Giselle later. I grab a bat, and jog up to home plate. I stare across the field and up at the scoreboard. We're still winning: 7-0. Two Outs. Bases loaded.

Beneath the scoreboard, a figure emerges from the woods. Mallory walks towards the field, auburn hair blowing back (Is it even that windy?), her green eyes fixated on me.

Suddenly, there's two of her. My vision fogs, and I sway on my feet. I look down, clench my eyes shut, and open them again. Home plate comes into focus.

What's wrong with me? Palms soaked in sweat; my bat is slippery in my hands. My heart beats out of rhythm. My lungs scream for air, but as deep as I inhale, I can't seem to fill them up. As the pitcher winds up, I'm seeing double again. Two balls, three balls, and then four balls sail into the air.

"Let's go, Saria! Bring me home," Keisha shouts from second base.

I swing haphazardly, not sure which ball to aim for. As my body twists, I lose my balance. I stagger, my arms flailing in the air. Everything happens in slow motion as I flounder through space, desperately trying to right myself, and fail. With a loud smack, I hit the ground, my cheek smacking against home plate, my hair in the dirt. The entire stadium is silent. It's the first time I wished that I had the power to disappear.

"Saria!" Coach kneels by my side. "Are you okay?"

I'm not okay. Nothing like this has ever happened before. I lift my head. The stadium is silent. In the bleachers, Penny's eyes are wide with concern, her hand over her mouth. A few seats down, my eyes lock with Mallory's. She smirks and learns forward, like a cat watching a cornered mouse, gleeful before she pounces on her prey. I blink and her expression is neutral. Am I seeing things?

I dig my palm into the dirt, using every ounce of energy to push myself up. My arms give out and I flop back to the ground. Thud! A hush falls over the crowd. Mallory winks; one green eye opens and shuts so fast that I can't be sure if I imagined it. Is Mallory somehow doing this to me? That's impossible, I tell myself. When did I become so paranoid?

Just then, an enormous crow swoops down, as if materializing from thin air. I cover my face as the crow dives towards me, its talons grazing my jersey as it shoots by. This is all too weird.

"Damn bird!" Coach says. "Saria, are you hurt?"

I grit my teeth, newfound determination taking root. "I'm okay." I rise to my feet, and lift my bat. My legs are jelly. and the bat feels like it's made of concrete, but I'm not giving up. The pitcher releases the ball. I swing too late.

"Strike two!"

I've never struck out before. Maybe I should just miss the next one on purpose. Strike out for the first time. Admit to the world that I'm not infallible. It might even make Giselle feel better. I could give her a moment to shine.

This would be the perfect time to do it. After all, we're winning. One strike out wouldn't affect the outcome of the game.

I reach underneath my Panther's jersey, and pull out my necklace. I hold the crystal pendant in between my fingers, feeling it heat up in my palm. Tears well up in my eyes. My entire self-worth revolves around being the best. Saria wins. It's what I'm known for. It's become my identity.

The pitcher throws the ball down the strike zone. I swing my bat hard. The ball soars over the pitcher's head, past the center fielder, and over the fence. Grand slam.

The crowd jumps to their feet and roars as I trot around the bases. At home plate, I'm mauled by hugs and hi-fives. My teammates hoist me up on their shoulders. "Saria! Saria! Saria!" They chant.

I should feel amazing, but instead, I'm on the verge of tears. "Saria! Saria! Saria!" What if I didn't have any powers?

Would I be good at anything? "Saria! Saria! Saria!" It's better to be fake than a loser, right?

I'm still bouncing on my teammates shoulders when I gaze across the field. In the bleachers, fans rise to their feet. "Saria! Saria! Saria!" Penny jumps up and down, clapping her hands overhead. The applause is deafening. Only one person remains seated, her lips curved into a sneer. Mallory.

Chapter Five

Zoeli

Justin drives up the long driveway and stops at my front door. "Great practice tonight, Zoe. The new song you wrote is awesome. We're going to kill it at The Battle of the Bands!"

"Hell yeah!" As Justin's old Volvo clunks away, I plop down on the white wicker rocking chair on my front porch. A cool breeze whistles through my hair. I pull my notepad from my bag and start writing some more lyrics. I've been on a roll lately.

Something rustles in the bush beside me. Two yellow eyes peek between the leaves. With one sleek movement, a black cat jumps through the branches and leaps into my lap. "Hi, Batman!" Maybe an unconventional choice, but I named my cat Batman because there's something bat-like about his eyes. Also, since I can almost never find him at night, I imagine that he's out saving the world vigilante-style.

I hold Batman against my chest and stroke his soft black fur. He rubs his cheek against my shoulder and purrs.

Two bright streaks of light illuminate the dark driveway. I squint as Chad's Range Rover pulls in front of my house. Chad parks, jumps out of the car, and races around to open the door for Saria.

Saria steps outside, and Chad instantly wraps her in his arms and kisses her. Bile creeps up in my throat. "You're so beautiful," Chad mumbles, running his fingers through Saria's hair. I really want to barf. "You are the best softball player, too." Blech. Blarg. Gack. If I keep holding back, I might end up projectile vomiting all over both of them. That wouldn't be the worst thing in the world…

"Goodnight, Chad," Saria says, untangling from his embrace.

"You sure you can't hang out a little longer? I hate being away from you." I swallow hard. How can my sister be with him after what he did to me?

"I'm tired, Chad. I'm going to bed."

"Okay, okay. One more kiss." I can't take it anymore. I gag loudly, making a show of producing a series of grotesque retching noises.

Saria spins around, her hands on her hips. "What're you doing here? Spying on me?"

"I live here," I say. "In case you forgot."

"You should go, Chad. I think my sister's sick."

"Goodnight, Saria. I love you." The driver door slams shut, and the SUV hums down the driveway.

Saria glares at me. "What was that all about?"

I'm about to give her a piece of my mind when Mom pops her head out the front door. "I thought I heard you girls. Come inside. We need to talk."

"Mom, I'm exhausted," Saria says.

"It's important." I'm not used to Mom using this tone. It sounds urgent. Fearful, even.

We follow Mom past the kitchen, down the long hallway, and into the "magic room." Wall-to-wall shelves are filled with crystals, herbs, live plants, and spell books. Saria maneuvers around the massive cauldron and sprawls out on the couch on the far side of the room. When we were kids, we used to meet here once a week for "magic lessons" with Mom. Other witches are invited to attend Enchantments Academy, but not us. Our family isn't welcome.

I sit in the oversized armchair in the opposite corner of the room, as far from Saria as possible. "Mom, are you feeling better?" I ask.

"I'm still tired, but I'm getting stronger," Mom says. "I'm sorry I missed your game, Saria. I just woke up."

"It's okay," Saria says. "We won." She offers a smile.

"No one cares," I snap, before I have a chance to stop myself.

"Zoe!" Mom scolds me. "Whatever is going on between the two of you, it's been going on far too long. You both need to get past it."

"What happened last night, Mom?" I change the subject. "Why were you so weak this morning?"

Mom sighs. "There was a girl about your age who got in a bad car accident. Her parents were hysterical. I couldn't help but think of how I would feel if it were one of you…"

Mom often uses her healing powers while working as an ER nurse. Sometimes, she takes it a little too far. If a witch uses too much magic at once, they can go into shock and die. In the witching world, they call it Magic Overuse Shock Syndrome, or MOSS. It's one of the first lessons Mom taught us when we were five.

"Mom, you need to be careful!" I say. Healing is one of the most strenuous forms of magic. It can lead to MOSS one hundred times faster than other uses of magic.

"I know my limits, Zoe. Don't worry about me," Mom says. "That's not why I called you in here tonight. There's something that I need to talk to you about. You girls may be in danger. We all may be."

I think of the guy in the woods, and my heart beats faster. I got away from him this time. Next time I might not be so lucky

"My sister called this evening. I haven't heard from her in almost a decade, not since…" Mom's voice drifts off.

I remember the incident like it was yesterday. Aunt Gwenna loomed over me, her shadow casting a darkness that shrouded my child-sized body. She pushed her glasses down the bridge of her beak-like nose, studying me like I was some kind of science experiment. She leaned forward, her lipstick-red mouth almost touching my ear as she rasped "Dirty little half-breed."

"What the hell did she want?" I ask.

"She wanted to warn us–"

"Ha!" I cut her off. "Since when does she give a damn about us?"

"She does care," Mom says. "There's a lot more to the story than you know."

"Then tell us!" Saria says. "Stop keeping things from us that we need to know!"

"It's complicated," Mom says. "I didn't want to upset or scare you. And I hate talking about it. I try to never think about it." Her voice breaks. "Because it hurts so much."

"Mom, if we could be in danger…" I say.

Mom takes a deep breath. "The crown." Mom lifts up her pant leg, revealing the three-pointed crown on her ankle. I run my fingers over the same mark on my wrist. "It means that we are royals."

I nod. We know the term, but not what it means. When Saria and I were little, we used to dress up like princesses and wait for the princes to come rescue us. "We're royals," we would say, swirling around in bell skirts. The princes never showed up, but we didn't care. We had each other.

"There are seven royal families," Mom says, "but only one family is appointed leaders of Aurelia. For decades, the Crowes were the rulers of the magical kingdom. We made the laws. We held the highest honors. My parents were king and queen, and my sister Gwenna and I were princesses."

"What?" I can't believe my ears. When Saria and I were small, Mom used to read us bedtime stories about Aurelia, but I'd always assumed it was a fictional place. "Aurelia is real?"

Mom nods. "I grew up there. In the royal castle."

"What was it like?"

"Some parts were amazing," Mom says. "All of the little girls looked up to me. I loved visiting them at school. I felt like I was making a difference, helping them fill their hearts with love and strive to use their powers for good. But there were lots of expectations and so many rules. I wasn't allowed to question the rules, even ones that were clearly rooted in prejudice. When I spoke up, I was accused of disrespecting tradition. They told me to shut up."

Mom takes a deep breath that shakes on its way out. "Then I broke the most sacred rule of all. I married a human. My entire family disowned me. They hoped that distancing themselves from me would help them circumvent the consequences." Mom wrings her hands. "When the seven royal families met to determine how to move forward, they decided that because of my parents 'failure,'" Mom uses air quotes, "to instill royal values in their children, they would be dethroned. I brought disgrace upon my family name, and they were forced to move out of the castle immediately."

"It wasn't your fault. You can't help who you fall in love with."

"I wish that was the end of it," Mom sighs. "It gets worse. Much worse."

Across the room, Saria is perched on the edge of the couch. She grips a throw pillow, her knuckles ghost-white. When she notices that I'm watching her, she looks the other way.

"Everyone was furious," Mom continues. "But my Uncle Talon took it the hardest. He was the Duke of Aurelia, and he reveled in the role, the power it afforded him. When my dad was removed as king, Talon felt that he was the rightful heir to the throne. After another royal family was appointed ruler of Aurelia, he was enraged..." Mom's voice trails off. "Talon always had a dark side, a side that was angry and hungry for power. There were many nights I heard my father and Talon arguing, especially about policies that protect humans. Talon supported political fringe groups who advocated for Aurelia's supernatural army to invade the human realm. During that time, my father was able to keep him in check by reminding him that insubordination could lead to his demotion."

"When he lost his title, he had nothing left to lose." A gust of wind blows through the open window. On a crystal table, an open spell book's pages rustle. Mom shivers. "He radicalized further, filling his empty heart with hate for others. As he rose within a brutal terrorist organization, he became addicted to the power, the reverence given to him by his followers. But it wasn't enough. He wanted more. He wanted to be the ruler, not only of the magical realm, but the human realm as well. His group called for the enslavement of all humans."

"The story gets uglier from there." Tears pool in her eyes. "I'll spare you the gruesome details, but please be careful. Aurelia's Intelligence team suspects that Talon and his militia are back. If they're plotting an attack, we're a top target."

My heart thumps. "Mom, there was a guy in the woods behind school." My voice comes out shaky. I feel dizzy as I struggle to catch my breath.

Mom's eyes widen. "Who? Did he hurt you?"

"I ran away. He knew my name. He was following me. I'm sure of it."

"Don't go anywhere alone," Mom says. "Have you noticed any boys following you?" Mom turns to Saria.

Saria smirks. "All the time."

I groan, suppressing the urge to punch her in the face. "Your pathetic followers can't save you from this."

"Okay, enough," Mom says. "It's late, and I'm exhausted. I'm going to bed." She closes the window, and clicks the lock shut. "I've done several protection spells on the house and the surrounding woods, but I can't be sure that they'll hold. Not against an evil so strong."

Outside, the wind howls. A tree branch scratches against the window, and my heart jumps into my throat. How am I going to sleep tonight?

Not too many years ago, whenever I had a nightmare, I would climb into Saria's bed. She would hold me, and we would fall asleep like that, all twisted up in each other's arms. That was before she betrayed me.

I stand up. "Goodnight," I say, heading to my room. The stairs creak under my feet, echoing against the narrow walls. But nothing echoes louder than the void in my heart.

Chapter Six

Saria

My phone buzzes. *Hey, we're outside.*

I look at the clock. 5pm.

It's kind of late for a hike, don't you think? I have to be back by 7pm.

Hikes at dusk are so much fun. Don't worry. It won't take long.

I grumble and stretch my arms overhead as I stand up. After the game and the talk with mom last night, I spent the entire day lounging on the couch, watching mindless reality TV. I'm still not sure how to process everything I learned.

As I slip on my sneakers, I wonder if I should even be going out in the woods. Mom told us to be careful. I open the front door, shaking my head as if to ward off my thoughts. I'm not going alone. I'll be fine.

As I approach Giselle's car, Penny jumps out of the passenger door. "Do you want to sit up front, Saria?"

"No thanks," I say, pulling open the back door.

"Are you sure?" Penny asks. "I really don't mind." She steps away from the car.

I hold out my palm. "Penny, really, I'm fine." I use a stern tone so she'll stop. Sometimes I wish my thrall didn't have this effect on her. There's two sides to this coin. On one hand, I have a friend who's loyal and will do anything for me. I'm grateful for that. But is our friendship even real? If I lost my powers tomorrow, would she still be my friend?

I slide into the backseat next to Keisha. "What are you rushing back for?" Giselle asks.

"I'm going to Logan's. We're doing a science project together."

"Oh, that's right." In the rearview mirror, I see Penny wrinkle her nose. "Are you going to miss Tony's party?"

I shrug. "I'm going to be late."

"Is Chad mad?"

"Chad isn't my keeper," I snap. Truthfully, Chad's super annoyed with me, and made me promise to be done by nine o'clock. "What's so great about Chad anyway?"

"You can't be serious," Giselle says. "He's loyal and gorgeous. He's the perfect boyfriend."

"He's hot, but he's controlling and full of himself. I don't get the hype." Keisha's arm hangs out the car window, beams of golden sun reflecting on her brown skin.

Keisha's right. Chad may be gorgeous, but he's far from perfect. His road rage is so bad that he followed a car that cut him off for thirty-minutes just to flip off the driver. His mom still does his laundry, and he thinks that every woman who claimed #metoo is a liar seeking personal gain.

And everyone seems to have forgotten what he did to Zoeli. But that was so many years ago, and he told me that he'd matured and changed. When he apologized, Zoeli said he was insincere. I thought that she was just jealous that he liked me and not her. Why did I assume the right to forgive him on her behalf? And then date him? Looking back, I made a lot of mistakes. Dimples and muscles can make a girl stupid, but that's not any excuse.

"He can have almost any girl in school, but he loves YOU, Saria. He follows you around like a lost puppy dog. You don't appreciate anything." Giselle's voice has an edge to it that reminds me of her tone at the game last night. When did she become so resentful towards me?

Giselle turns the radio up. My eardrums might rupture, but at least this conversation is over. I watch out the window, trees whizzing by in blurs of green and orange when a sharp pain stabs me in the forehead. My body curls forward. I press my hands to my head and suppress a scream. I gag as a wave of nausea washes over me. Giselle's car sputters up the unpaved path, tiny rocks dinging against the sides.

As soon as she rolls to a stop, I fling open my door and stumble outside. I rest my hands on my knees, dry heaving as I inhale the crisp autumn air.

"Are you okay?" Penny is beside me, her hand on my back. *Am I okay?*

The back of my neck prickles. I'm overcome by that strange feeling again, a sense that someone is watching me. I glance over my shoulder. A small crescent of sun peeks out from behind the mountain, only a few rays stretching over to illuminate the rocky structure. It's already getting dark.

As quickly as they came on, my symptoms subside. *What's wrong with me?* "I'm a little carsick, I guess." Giselle's car is all alone in the parking lot. The wind blows, and a cluster of leaves scatter across the empty space. I shiver and reach into my pocket, checking my phone. "No reception."

"There never is," Giselle says.

Penny stands next to me, her eyes wide with concern. Keisha waits with Penny, but Giselle is already a few yards ahead. "Do you feel up to hiking?" Keisha asks. Giselle steps onto the trail bordering the parking lot. A moment later, she disappears into the thicket.

"I'm okay," I say. "Let's go." I don't realize how fast I'm walking until I hear Penny panting beside me. "Giselle!" I shout. "Where are you?"

I hear footsteps, leaves crunching underneath the weight of someone's feet. "Giselle?" Keisha says. There's no response.

Penny grabs my hand, her palm clammy against mine. I'm not supposed to use magic in front of my human friends, but a life-or-death situation is an exception. Hopefully it doesn't come down to that.

I crane my neck, peering behind a pile of rocks. "Boo!" I jump and spin, raising the hand that isn't holding Penny's, prepared to zap whoever's there with a burst of magic.

Giselle doubles over with laughter. "You should see your faces!" She can barely get the words out between fits of laughter. "Let's play hide-and-seek! Saria, you're it!"

The sky is darkening by the minute. I remember what Mom said last night. We need to be careful. "Let's stick together."

"Oh, come on, Saria," Giselle points to a large oak. "Put your head against the tree and count to ten."

"I don't think that's a good idea," I say.

"I second that," Keisha says.

"Why? We played all the time when we were kids." Giselle smiles. It's been a long time since I've seen her smile like that: wide, carefree and child-like. It reminds me of simpler times: when Giselle, Zoeli, and I were three peas in a pod. Before we were worried about who got the boy or who played better in the game. I want to feel like that again.

An evil great uncle, royal witches, supernatural militias…none of it feels real. Mom's warning seems to fade as quickly as the sun rays are swallowed up behind the mountain. One quick game of hide-and-seek won't put anyone in danger.

"Fine," I grumble.

"Are you insane?" Keisha puts her hands on her hips. "There could be serial killers in these woods."

"Come on, just one game," Giselle says.

Keisha sighs. "Remind me why I'm friends with you again."

Giselle slings her arm over Keisha's shoulder. "I bring out your adventurous side."

"If I end up on the dead side, I'm coming back to haunt your adventurous ass."

"I'll stay with you," Penny says, looping her arms through Keisha's. Penny's eyes are wide, her gaze darting from tree to tree. She's not only offering to stay together for Keisha's benefit.

"It's decided then." Giselle grins triumphantly. "Let's play." She slides a hairband off her wrist and pulls her brown curls up into a messy bun.

I turn and rest my head against the tree. "One Mississippi, Two Mississippi." Giselle squeals with excitement. "Three Mississippi, Four Mississippi." Footsteps thud and then disappear as my friends run out of earshot. "Five Mississippi. Ready or not, here I come!"

A loud cackle echoes through the trees. I freeze. None of my friends laugh like that– cruel and mocking. I spin around, but I don't see anyone.

Acorns pop and twigs snap beneath my sneakers. I peek behind rocks and trees, but I don't see a soul. The stillness is almost eerie. These girls are good.

A shriek cuts through the night. I stop short. "Giselle?" No one answers. "Guys, this isn't funny!" A cloud passes over the sun, shrouding the woods in darkness. Another shrill scream reverberates through the trees, coming from deep within the thicket. "Penny! Giselle! Come out! If this is your idea of a joke…" I step over a rock, leaving the trail behind.

Someone darts between the trees, auburn hair flying behind her. "Mallory!" I shout. "Why are you here?" As quickly as she appeared, she's gone.

I weave my way between rocks, trees, and thorn bushes. Thorns snag my t-shirt, ripping the thin fabric. I pull the prickers out, thorns piercing my palm, blood dripping down my wrist.

"Come out guys!" I shout. "This isn't funny!" I sound like a broken record. A light shower falls from the sky, pitter-pattering against leaves. The forecast said it would be sunny and clear. I should never trust the weather report. "Guys, let's go!" I shout again. A gust of wind blows, whistling through a maze of bark and branches.

Rain falls faster now, pelting my face. I shudder, wrapping my arms around myself, wishing I'd worn a jacket. "Come out, come out, wherever you are!" Thunder cracks. Rain pours down in sheets. I hear laughter again: evil, taunting. "Who are you?" I shout, but the wind drowns out my voice. My hair is plastered to my scalp, streams of water dripping down my face.

The wind picks up. It's like I'm caught in a cyclone. Leaves, rain, and bark swirl around me. Another gale knocks me off balance. I stumble, nearly falling before I cling to a tree trunk.

Above me, I hear a loud crack. I look up, squinting against the wind and rain. Branches strain and bend against the hurricane-force winds. I don't have time to move. The biggest bough crashes down on me.

A world of pain envelops me as I'm knocked to the ground. Pinned beneath the enormous branch, I howl in agony. Someone cackles again. This time, the sound is loud and clear, vibrating in my brain, thrumming my eardrums, as though it's coming from inside me.

My chest throbs. I place my hand over my heart and discover that I've been impaled by an offshoot of the gigantic bough. If I was a vampire, I'd be a cloud of smoke. "Help!" I shout. "Help me!"

It feels like hours that I'm lying there, writhing in pain, drowning in the torrential rains. The world is fading in and out when I notice three figures looming over me.

"Saria! Are you okay?" Giselle's hand covers her mouth.

"Someone call 911!" Penny's lip quivers, like she might cry.

"There's no service." Keisha looks at her phone.

"I'll run and get help," Mallory says.

"You goddamn won't!" I slide onto my forearms, my elbows sinking into the mud. The rain has slowed to a drizzle. "What the hell are you doing here?"

Mallory's brows push together. "Giselle told me you guys were out here. I came to meet up."

"You did this to me!" I gesture to the jagged piece of wood protruding from my chest.

Mallory's mouth opens. "You're not making any sense."

I realize that I sound insane, but I can't stop myself. "This is your fault!" I shout again. "If you think I'm going to trust you to call for help, you're out of your mind!"

Keisha kneels beside me. "Saria, calm down. What are you talking about?"

"She's crazy," Mallory says, and rolls her eyes.

"Stop! Just stop arguing! Saria needs help!" Penny says. At least I have one true friend. "I'll run until I get service, and then I'll call 911."

I shake my head. "I'll be okay. Just help me get this thing off me."

Giselle examines my wound. "We need to go to the hospital. If we try to remove it, we could make it worse."

"How am I going to get to a hospital? Half of a tree is on top of me!"

"We'll call the paramedics. They'll come out here and remove it the right way," Keisha says.

I wave her away. "It looks worse than it is. It barely scratched the surface." I'm lying, but I'd rather go home and ask Mom to heal me. It'll be faster and won't leave a scar. "Now help me."

Giselle shakes her head, and takes a few steps back. "This isn't a good idea."

"Help me," I repeat, locking eyes with Penny. She hesitates for a moment, and then kneels beside me. She wraps her fingers around the branch.

"I thought we'd reached the height of stupidity." Keisha shakes her head in disbelief. "But it turns out that we can go even higher."

"This is going to hurt." Mallory says, squatting beside the heaviest part of the bough.

"Don't look so happy about it," I mutter.

Mallory makes a face. She grabs the bough, her fingernails digging into the bark. "On the count of three. One. Two. Three." As I push, Mallory and Penny lift.

"Argghh!" The dagger twists, taking a chunk of my flesh with it on the way out. Blood gushes from a gaping hole in my chest. Giselle's mouth drops open in horror.

Penny clenches her eyes shut. "I can't look! I faint at the sight of blood."

On the other hand, Mallory seems to perk up. She wears a wolflike expression as she watches my blood pour down, a sticky mixture of dirt, blood and grime puddling beneath me.

Giselle pulls her shirt over her head, and presses it against my wound. "We need to keep pressure on it," she says. "And get you to a doctor."

I stagger to Giselle's car, leaning on Keisha's shoulder, Penny's hands clamped around my arm like a vise grip. "You're hurting me," I say.

Her eyes brim with tears. "I'm so sorry. I just want to keep you safe." I don't complain again.

I slide into the passenger seat. I ball up Giselle's shirt in my fists, and clasp it against my chest. My fingers are stained by blood. I close my eyes and channel my power, willing the bleeding to stop. It doesn't work. Healing yourself is harder than healing others. I don't have much practice with either.

"We're going to the hospital," Giselle says, turning onto the highway.

I clear my throat and focus on my magical energy, simmering in my core. "Take me home," I say, and I know she'll do it. I may not be good at healing others, but I've mastered controlling them. I used to think that was a good thing.

Something burns in the corners of my eyes. I can't be sure if it's rain, blood or tears. "I heard you laughing. I know you guys were messing with me."

"You're delusional." Mallory snickers. Her laugh reminds me of the cackle in the woods. Was it her?

"Mallory, stop," Giselle shivers in her bra, her knuckles white around the steering wheel. "I'm sorry, Sar. We were just joking around."

"Who's *we*?" Keisha says. "Because I'd like to make it clear that I wasn't involved in any of that foolery."

"Okay," Mallory seems to relent. "I'm sorry, too." Her apology doesn't sound as genuine as Giselle's. "But we didn't cause the tree to fall on you. We don't control the weather."

"I knew this was a bad idea, but no one listened to me." Keisha shakes her head. "Just one game, they said. It'll be fun, they said."

We don't control the weather. Mallory's voice rings in my ears. Are there witches powerful enough to command the weather? Even when I've tried my hardest, the most I can do is make the wind pick up a little. If there's witches who can summon tornadoes, what else are they capable of?

I shake my head. I'm losing it again. There's no such thing as witches who can conjure storms. It was just a freak natural occurrence. Right?

***

A half-hour later, I lay on the floor of the magic room, surrounded by healing crystals and candles. Mom kneels beside me, her hands cupped around my wound. I feel heat and tingles as she goes to work.

A few minutes later, Mom lifts her hands. "All done," she says, brushing her jeans as she stands up. I place my fingers where my wound was. The skin is smooth and soft, wholly intact. It's like nothing ever happened.

Mom hands me a damp towel and a bandage. "Keep a bandage on for at least a few weeks. Any sooner will rouse suspicion."

I wipe away the remaining blood and stick the bandage on. Most people use bandages to protect wounds while they heal. I use them to conceal evidence.

I always take short-cuts. I mend on the surface, but inside, I'm broken. The truth stays hidden.

"Now tell me what happened," Mom says. "Every detail."

"At first it was just a drizzle, but then the rain and wind were coming so fast," I shudder. "I was clinging to the tree trunk when a branch came down on me." I pause. "Mom, are there witches who can do that?"

Mom takes a deep breath. "It's possible. Especially if a few are working together."

I bring my knees to my chest, and wrap my arms around them. I rock gently in the fetal position. "I've had a feeling lately that someone is watching me," I say. "I'm not sure if it's paranoia or what, but I'm too nervous to walk to Logan's house tonight."

Mom raises her eyebrows. "Logan Archer? It's been a long time since I heard that name."

"He's my partner for a science project."

"He used to be one of your best friends."

I shrug. "We're still friends." Logan's house borders the forest that surrounds mine. Years ago, he lurked around the forest, always a few yards behind us. Zoe and I coined him, "the boy in the woods." Once he finally worked up the courage to say hi, we became friends. We probably explored every square inch of the forest together. We even discovered an old, abandoned graveyard. I grin, remembering when we tried to summon their spirits. Logan got so scared he tripped over a gravestone and fell face first in the mud.

That was long before I started dating Chad, way before everything got so complicated. Chad doesn't think it's cool to have friends of the opposite sex. Between Chad and sports, I didn't have much time left for Logan anyway.

"I always liked Logan," Mom says, her voice warm. "You should go. You seem down. He'll cheer you up."

"Is it safe?" I ask. "To walk through the woods to his house."

Mom stands up. "I'll drive you."

I almost protest, but then I remember that it's Logan. I don't have to be embarrassed to have Mom drop me off. "Okay." For the first time in days, my smile feels genuine.

***

"The first step is coming up with a question. Here's a few I thought of. Can a black light detect invisible stains? Do vitamins affect the growth of flowers?" Logan pauses. "What question would you like to find the answer to?"

I need answers to many questions, but none that can be solved by our science project. I want to know who my real friends are. I used to be so sure of Giselle's loyalty, but after the last softball game, I'm not so sure. I want to know who loves me for me, and who's entranced by my thrall. Most of all, I want to know what I'm capable of: where magic ends and I begin. Who I truly am.

Tears brim inside my eyes. Logan's face turns blurry. His forehead creases. "Is everything okay? You can talk to me about anything. You know that."

Tears threaten to escape. I struggle to hold onto the persona I've perfected: strong and beautiful. If I allow myself to cry, I'll show weakness. I won't look pretty with smeared makeup and puffy eyes.

But with Logan, it doesn't matter. I let it go. Tears slide down my face.

In the past, Logan was always there when I needed him. Even now, despite how I distanced myself these past few years, he reaches across the table and places his hand on top of mine. The tears flow faster, like a dam breaking.

Logan moves around the table, and slides into the chair beside me. "Saria, what's wrong?"

"I'm convinced that someone's been following me. Someone who wants to hurt me." Logan hands me a tissue. I wipe my eyes.

"Who would want to hurt you?" Logan's voice has an edge I haven't heard before: protective, angry.

"I don't know." I shake my head. "Sometimes I feel like I'm going crazy. I'm not sure if I know the difference between a friend and an enemy. It's like…" My voice drifts off, then comes back stronger. "It's like, I've been fake for so long I can't even tell what's real anymore." The confession feels cathartic, like a weight being lifted off my shoulders.

"Fake?" Logan's eyebrows bunch together. "What do you mean?"

I can't tell him about my powers. "It's hard to explain." I take a deep breath. "At first, I brought it on myself. I've always been competitive, but I think it was also my insecurities. It felt good to be a star. Now it's become my entire identity. I don't know who I am anymore."

Logan's fingers stroke my palm, and then interlock with mine. "I know who you are, Saria. You used to carry a bird-watching journal everywhere you went. By the time you logged over two-hundred species of birds, the pages were falling apart from being turned and creased so many times."

It's true that I've always felt connected with birds. Sometimes, when I watch them burst into flight, I'm compelled to lift my arms, as though some part of me expects to sprout wings and fly away. "I love how animals don't overthink things," I say. "They don't worry about what everyone else thinks of them."

As if on cue, fur presses against my leg. "Rambo!" I lean down to rub the cat's head.

"Remember when we found them in that old abandoned shed in the woods?"

"Of course I remember," I say. Zoe heard the meows first, but she wasn't strong enough to move the rusty, broken door. A little of my magic helped with that. Once we were inside the shed, we discovered the litter of kittens. A moment later, Logan appeared, always a few steps behind us.

"Seven tiny kittens," Logan recalls. "Abandoned by their mother. Sick, hungry and freezing cold. You saved them all. I still don't know how you did it."

I laugh. "It wasn't magic." And it really wasn't, I remember proudly. "I hand fed them around the clock. I wrapped them up in warm blankets."

"You slept on the ground with them. In the middle of winter. In below freezing temperatures." Logan says.

"Only for a couple of hours. Once my mom realized I was serious about sleeping in the snow, she let me bring them inside." I shake my head. "Dad had puffy eyes and a runny nose for weeks. If he wasn't allergic, we would've made Mom keep them all."

"I think Rambo has a pretty good home here," Logan says.

"He sure does." Rambo jumps in my lap and headbutts my chest, his purr vibrating against me. I look down at my hands: one embedded in Rambo's fur, the other intertwined with Logan's. It feels right.

"Saria, I care about you. If you need anyone, I'm always here."

"I know." And I do know. Or is Logan only bewitched as well? I blink back tears, my heart rising up in my throat. How will I ever know?

Logan slips off his glasses and places them on the table. His eyes are hazel: almost amber, surrounded by black lashes. "You have really nice eyes," I say, before I catch myself.

"Really?" Logan's cheeks turn red. For a moment, we're both quiet, staring at our interlocked hands. "It's been a tough day for you. Let's forget the science project for tonight. Want to just hang out and watch funny movies?"

My phone vibrates, and Chad's picture appears on the screen. "I actually have to go," I say, checking my watch. "Chad's picking me up."

Logan's smile drops, and he pulls his hand away.

"I'm sorry," I say, sliding out of my seat and answering the call.

"Where are you? I'm waiting outside Logan's house. It's nine o'clock."

"I'll be right there," I say, shrugging on my coat. I walk towards the door, and then turn to look back at Logan. His skinny frame is hunched over, hands deep in his pockets, his gaze on the floor. He shifts from foot to foot.

He's the polar opposite of the muscular, self-assured boy waiting outside in his overpriced luxury vehicle.

Yet, I don't want to leave. Before I can stop myself, I draw him in for a hug. I rest my head against his chest and feel his heart beating a million times per minute.

It hurts to pull away.

"Bye." I'm careful to avert my gaze as I open the front door. Outside, Chad's headlights blind me. I squint and raise my hand over my eyes. His horn blares, slicing through the night.

Logan is sweet and thoughtful and REAL. When he decides to give his heart to someone, his love will be patient and unselfish and gallant and everything that I'm not.

I leave because he deserves so much better than me.

Chapter Seven

Zoeli

The second hand on the wall clock ticks in slow motion as Ms. Miller's monotone drones on and on. Across the room, Chad stretches, exposing a strip of skin above his belt. Someone so disgusting shouldn't have abs like that. It isn't fair that our outsides don't align with our insides. The world would be a much better place if we knew right off the bat who people truly are.

The bell rings. "That was a nice nap." Yazmin lifts her head off the desk beside mine. "I can't stay awake to hear all the lies. Columbus was a deplorable man who enslaved and killed Native Americans. If Columbus was a woman, that wouldn't have happened. I can count on one hand how many women are mentioned in our textbook. Once we're on the suffrage movement, then I'll pay attention."

Yazmin follows my gaze across the room. "Gross." She wrinkles her nose. Yazmin will never forgive Chad for what he did to me.

It was years ago, but I remember it like it was yesterday. Complete and utter humiliation has a way of sticking with you like that.

After years of crushing on Chad, I finally built up the courage to ask him out. When he agreed to meet me at the movies, I was over the moon. Mom and Saria fussed over me, spending hours on my hair and makeup. We were all so excited. I'd been doodling his name all over my notebook since kindergarten. I thought maybe he'd even go to the eighth-grade dance with me.

When Mom dropped me off at the movie theater, he was waiting outside. When I slid into the seat beside him, my heart felt like it would burst from excitement. He said he was going to get popcorn and that he'd be right back. I smiled, imagining us both reaching into the same bucket of popcorn, his hand accidentally grazing mine.

He never returned.

But that wasn't the worst part.

Devastated, I wandered around the movie theater, calling his name, looking for him. Eventually, when I realized he was gone, I collapsed on the sidewalk outside, bawling my eyes out.

I didn't know he was right around the corner, recording me. A few hours later, the video of me crying was posted all over social media, with the caption "When you ditch the LOSER girl mid-date."

If that wasn't cruel enough, the comments from my classmates were worse. Everyone was laughing at me, reveling in my pain, insulting everything about me: my clothes, my body and face.

It was enough to break anyone. It didn't break me. In the end, it made me stronger. If no one likes me, that's fine. I know that I can still love myself.

At the time, Saria wanted to put a hex on him. Mom forbade it, saying that using black magic for vengeance violated magical laws.

I never imagined that two years later she would date him.

Yazmin swings her backpack over her shoulder. "I still can't believe that Saria's with that scumbag. She's gross, too."

"She doesn't care about anything but her stupid image." I turn down the hallway. "I'll see you at band practice."

I swing open my locker. On top of a stack of books, there's a large red envelope. My brow furrows as I rip it open. How did this get inside my locker? It's too large to fit through the slots.

The paper inside is yellowed and brittle with curling edges.

Evulsion

General Information: Evulsion is the act of forcibly removing magical energy from a witch without their consent. This practice should only be utilized as a punishment when a witch has been caught misusing their powers. Since witches will strongly resist the removal of their powers, the success of this spell depends on: the strength of the witch conducting the evulsion, the phase of the moon, and the amount of blood and hair used. Even a powerful witch under a full moon is not likely to evulse more than ten percent of another witch's powers.

<u>Warning!</u> Since evulsion is an "organ" transplant of sorts, it is essential that spell caster and the target witch are a match. Close relatives are likely compatible, but it is always wise to run a test prior to conducting an evulsion. Refer to page 578 for "Magical Compatibility Test" instructions. If the spell caster's and target witch's magical energy are not compatible, the spell caster's body may reject the energy, resulting in long-term illness. In severe cases, death may occur.

Even when compatible, magic should be evulsed gradually. If too much is taken at once, the spell caster may suffer severe illness and/or death.

<u>Ingredients:</u> Blood of target witch, Hair of target witch, Three black candles

    I gasp as I realize that I'm holding a page that's been ripped from its spell book. I may be an uneducated "half-breed," but even I know that spell books, especially ancient spell books, are sacred. Tearing them apart is strictly forbidden.

    My hands shake as I jam the page back into the envelope. Another slip of paper floats to the floor, staring up at me, its message scrawled in black marker.

You don't have to be the weaker sister

A cold sweat breaks along my hairline. I look over my shoulder. The hallways are packed: students moving this way and that, laughing and giving high-fives, happy to end their day. No one seems to notice me. I ball up the slip of paper and stuff it in my pocket.

Who put this in my locker? Who knows our secret? I think of the guy who appeared in the woods behind school. Did he have something to do with this?

I sort through my messy locker, finding the books I need for homework. I slam my locker shut and head outside. The parking lot is empty.

A security guard leans against a pillar. "Where are the buses?" I ask.

"Gone," he says.

"Already?" I check my watch. I'm a few minutes later than usual, but well within the time frame to catch the bus.

"The bus drivers seemed in a rush today," the security guard says. "Now that you mention it, it was a bit odd, the way they corralled everyone and then zoomed on out of here."

"Great," I mutter. I'm sure Saria got a ride with Chad or one of her many minions. I'll just walk home. I strongly doubt that witch militias attack on the street in broad daylight. Still, I glance over my shoulder twice as the school disappears over the hill.

The roads are quieter than I expected. Birds chirp. Trees rustle. An errant plastic bag is trapped up in branches. It billows and snaps against the breeze.

I pick up my pace. I want to get home. A cloud drifts over the sun, hiding half its light. I'm breathing heavily now, moving faster with each step.

The sky darkens as more clouds move through. I have the strangest feeling that someone is watching me. I look over my shoulder, but no one is there.

The black Escalade stirs up pebbles as it rolls up beside me. My heart launches into my throat as the tinted window descends.

I want to run, but I can't. It's as if my feet are glued to the sidewalk. First, there's black hair, thick and wavy. Thick brows. Long black eyelashes. And those eyes. Darker and deeper and even more intense than I remembered.

"Zoeli, don't run," he says. I try to scream but it gets caught in my throat. It feels like someone jammed a chicken bone in my trachea. "I didn't want to use magic on you, but you have to let me explain." I'm frozen like a statue as he unbuttons his shirt. I try to look away, but my neck won't move. He opens his shirt, revealing perfectly defined pecs. I can't be sure if I'm being forced to stare anymore. My heart might explode from beating so hard.

"I'm Damian." He pulls his undershirt aside and reveals the mark: a five-pointed crown. "I'm a royal. Please don't scream."

I cough and sputter as my voice returns. "What do you want?" I'm free to move again. I step back.

Damian holds his hands up. "I won't hurt you. Royals look out for each other. Our families made oaths. You can trust me."

"Uncle Talon was a royal. He tried to kill my parents."

He shakes his head. "Talon's insane. He's not like the rest of us."

"Really? And what are the rest of you like? Do you mean the rest of you who persecuted and exiled my mother for loving my father? Or the rest of you who object to my very existence?" I shake my head in disgust. "Forgive me if your stupid crown doesn't inspire my unequivocal trust."

"Fair point." Damian swings his head around, his eyes intent as he watches out the back window. I follow his gaze, but all I see are trees swaying.

Something darts behind a bush. It happens so fast that I can't make out its form: only a white flurry of movement. Was that an animal? Or is someone hiding, waiting to strike?

"You're in danger. Please get in the car."

"I don't take rides with strangers," I say. Even gorgeous strangers with really nice pecs who claim they're protecting me. I have to give him credit. The offer's hella tempting.

The car door slams and then he's charging at me. I clench my fists and raise them, a defensive pose I learned in kickboxing class. I don't stand a chance against him, but if I'm going down, then I'm going down fighting.

Damian looks mildly amused. "Zoeli, darling, if I was going to force you into my car, you'd already be inside, and I wouldn't have to physically engage with you."

A chill rushes through my veins. He sounds so confident in his ability to control me. No one should have that much power. I imagine myself as his puppet; as he manipulates the strings, my wooden mouth snaps open and slams shut, a manufactured grin chiseled on my face, his laughter ringing in my ears.

"You don't have to worry about that. We aren't allowed to use mind-control unless we're in imminent danger." Can he read my mind? My cheeks turn hot. I hope he couldn't see my thoughts when he unbuttoned his shirt, because that would be super embarrassing. "I'm a royal," he continues. "I know what's expected of me. I follow the rules." He pauses. "Most of the time. I've learned from my mistakes."

"Unlike my mother," I mutter, folding my arms, walking away as fast as I can. Where are all the cars? It's rush hour, but the streets are empty. Should I call the cops? I don't think the police academy trains officers in mind-control resistance and supernatural defense. I'm only a mile away from home. I just want to get there safely.

Damian falls in step beside me. "What are you doing?" I ask

"I thought that was fairly obvious. Since you won't get in my car, I'm walking you home. I'm protecting you."

"I can take care of myself." This isn't true, and I know it, but something about this random guy assuming that I'm a damsel in distress who needs a big strong man to save me bothers me and brings out my feminist side. Yaz would be proud.

"You don't know what you're up against," he says. "Talon's militia has grown larger and stronger. His followers are more demented, evil, and powerful than anything you've ever imagined."

"And what are you going to do? Single handedly take on a supernatural army?"

Damian raises his brows. "Don't underestimate my skills."

"Don't underestimate mine," I bite back. We walk in silence for a few moments. My heart races. I'm not sure if my imagination's running wild, but I have the sudden intuition that evil is all around us, closing in. The trees become cages, their branches like claws, threatening to trap me. "What's the plan?" I ask. "If they attack us."

"They won't," Damian says. "They won't mess with me." He sounds so confident.

"Why are they afraid of you?" I wish I could stop my damn voice from shaking.

"Let's just say…" Something howls in the woods. The road is so quiet I can hear the leaves rustling on the pavement as the wind blows through. "I'm well connected."

I would love to smack that smirk off his face. If given the chance, Damian and Saria would probably fall madly in love. They could spend their whole lives boasting about their incredible powers and social stature. That's not my jam. "Would you care to elaborate? Forgive my ignorance, but since your kind forbade me from attending your exclusive Enchantments Academy, and banished my entire family from your realm, I'm a bit out of the loop."

He's so much bigger than me. Looking up to study his face, I squint at the sun. He stares straight ahead, his jaw clenched. I don't know if I should be scared of him, or whatever else is out there. Maybe I should watch what I say.

There's a long pause. "Half-breeds don't need to be educated in the magical arts. Your powers are so diluted that you wouldn't be able to pass our classes."

In a way, I think he's right. My powers are for the birds. But I'm way too proud to admit that to him. "Hmph." I kick some pebbles on the ground. "You should see what my sister Saria can do. She would've aced all your classes. Even without formal instruction, she's one bad-ass witch." I can't believe I'm bragging about my sister, but hey, desperate times, desperate measures. I'm not going to stand here and let him insult an entire group of people. Besides, if I'd been allowed in their schools, maybe I would've learned how to connect with my magical energy. Mom always said that I gave up too early. When I saw that I couldn't compete with Saria, I kind of stopped trying. Instead, I focused on my passion, music.

Damian raises his brows. "A half-breed ace our classes? I think not. Maybe you'd do alright in history, and even pass a paper test on theory, but you'd fail every hands-on exam."

"So, you think you're superior to me?"

"I don't think. I know."

My fists clench at my sides. I'm fighting every fiber in my being to restrain myself from clocking this guy in the face. I don't care if he has the power to stop the world from turning, I'll out-strum him on my guitar any day of the week. And even though I've only spoken with him for a few minutes, it's fair to say that I would destroy him in sensitivity, empathy, and intelligence.

"But I don't see any harm in you learning our history. After all, you are half-witch. I can understand that you would want to know where that part of you came from."

"Oh, thank you dear superior master for deeming me worthy enough to learn my own history!" My voice drips with sarcasm.

"You're welcome," he quips, grinning down at me.

"You're not cute," I say, wishing it wasn't a lie. I pick up my pace.

"Hey, don't get mad at me," he says, speeding up to my side. "That's what they teach us in school."

I don't respond. There's no point in engaging with indoctrinated idiots. I can't wait to get home and never see this loser again in my life.

"I can teach you," he says.

"In case you're unaware, half-breeds are literate. It's unbelievable, I know. Against all odds, I've learned to read! I think I'll educate myself, thank you very much."

"Ahh, that is impressive," he says. "But I'll teach you what you can't find in any textbook. The real dirt."

"On what?" I raise my brows.

"We can start with the royals."

"What about them?" I try to sound bored and disinterested. I don't want to give him the satisfaction of knowing he's piqued my interest.

"Did you know that the Crowes weren't the first royal family to be dethroned?"

"No, I didn't know that." The wind blows; a flurry of leaves blast towards me. Damian lifts his palms up. The leaves stop mid-air, and then drop to the ground one-by-one.

I step over them and keep walking. "You're welcome," he says, his bottom lip stuck out in a pout.

"Thank you so much for rescuing me from those scary leaves!" I flail my arms dramatically. "I'm just a frail half-breed, so who knows what kind of damage they could've done to my weak and decrepit self? They might have even messed up my hair! You're my hero! What can I ever do to repay you?"

"You're forever indebted to me, for sure." Damian grins. "And since I'm feeling so charitable towards the misfortunate today, I might even share a tale that you won't find in any textbooks."

"Enlighten me."

"When the royal families were first established, the Crowes weren't the original leaders. The Wolfes were the first family to rule Aurelia. They reigned for hundreds of years, until one of their daughters made a grave mistake."

"Did she fall in love with a human?"

"Nope, she had far bigger plans."

"What could be bigger than finding your true love and starting a family?"

"Eternal life, infinite power, and world domination."

I shrug. "To each their own."

"Licinia Wolfe became a vampire."

"A what?" I didn't mean for my voice to sound so shrill. My cheeks heat up.

"Your mom never told you about vampires?" Damian sighs. "We're going to have to start with the basics."

"She did," I say. Sort of. When we were younger, during one of our "lessons," Mom mentioned vampires. When Saria cried, Mom assured us that vampires wouldn't hurt us, and never mentioned them again. "She said that they're a dying race."

"Well, not exactly," Damian says. "Because they don't die. They're immortal. But she's right that there are very few of them left in this world. We killed most of them." He says this last part with some kind of sick pride.

"We killed them?"

"It wasn't without cause. Witch's blood is irresistible to vampires, making us natural enemies." Damian pauses. "For hundreds of years, we lived in fear. Vampires would capture witches and throw parties. They'd all gather for the feast, dressed to the nines for the special occasion. We were considered a delicacy."

"That's horrible," I say.

"That's why we had to put a stop to it. They started the war, but we finished it. Unfortunately, there were many casualties. Rest easy to my brothers and sisters who sacrificed their lives." Damian kisses his fingertips and touches the sky. "The remaining vampires made an agreement with the royal family. The pact forbade them from drinking the blood of witches, and from creating any new vampires. Both parties signed, and then there was peace. They stayed out of our way, and we stayed out of theirs.

"For almost a hundred years, they followed the rules. Then, Licinia Wolfe came along. Even though she was poised to become queen, that wasn't enough for her. She was hungry for more power. Although very few witches have successfully transitioned to vampires over the history of our kind, those who survive the transition are some of the most powerful creatures on earth.

"Years ago, a vampire scientist ran an experiment to see how many witches he could turn into vampires. Less than one percent made it. The rest died. He killed over three hundred witches during his studies."

"Why would he continue the experiment when so many already died?" I ask.

"Vampires don't care about taking lives. To them, killing a witch is the same as you or I stepping on a bug."

"It can't be that every vampire feels that way."

Damian huffs. "You're wrong. Real-life vampires aren't anything like the silly sparkly ones on your human tv. They're vicious and cunning and if they believe there will not be a consequence, they will not hesitate to kill you." Damian steps on my front porch. "You're home safe. You see? I'm not that bad. Maybe we could even be friends."

"I don't make a habit of befriending people who think they're above me." I place my hand on the front door handle. Part of me is disappointed that our time has come to an end. Just because of the history lesson though. Nothing to do with him.

"Until we meet again, Zoeli." His voice softens. "Stay safe."

I step inside and turn around, my hand up to wave. He's gone. My hand falters, then slowly drops by my side. I look in every direction, but he's nowhere to be found. It's like he disappeared into thin air.

I close the door and lock it behind me, my heart rattling inside my rib cage. Who is he? WHAT is he? Can full-blood witches just vanish like that? I need answers.

Down the hallway, I creak open the door to the magic room. The walls are lined with shelves displaying dozens of books that Mom collected over the years. I skim the titles, "Fundamentals of Magical Healing," "Rare Potions," "Enchanted Herbs and Plants."

"Ahh, here we go." I slide a textbook titled "History of Aurelia: Volume 1" off the shelf.

Crash! Bang! Startled, I drop the book. It hits the floor like a brick. A cloud of dust swirls around my feet.

A huge crow slams against the window, again and again. If that wasn't horrifying enough, there's something wrapped around the crow, a piece of fabric that appears to be covered in blood.

It collides into the window again, this time so hard that its beak cracks the glass.

I scream.

Chapter Eight

Saria

When I hear my sister scream, I burst into action. Without hesitation, without forethought, I'm there for her. I'm ready to fight an army of supernatural creatures if I have to. They better not lay a finger on Zoe.

Mom and I arrive in the doorway of the magic room at the same time. Zoe is pale as a ghost, pointing at the window.

A crow crashes into the broken glass window; eyes bulging as it squawks loudly, as though it's angry at us. I've never seen anything like it. I lift my palm up, ready to zap it back to wherever it came from.

Mom grabs my hand, "No!"

"What?" I ask. "We're allowed to use magic in self-defense. Clearly this bird's gone wild and is trying to hurt us."

Mom shakes her head. "You don't understand." Instead of moving away, she opens the window. The bird flies inside and perches on the arm of the couch.

Mom folds her arms across her chest. "Gwenna! What the hell's wrong with you? We have a front door! You're paying for that window."

With a burst of black feathers, Aunt Gwenna materializes on the couch, holding a piece of blood-stained pink cotton. It takes a moment to register that it's Giselle's shirt, and it's covered in MY blood. She waves it in the air. "You idiots! You threw this away in the regular garbage! Do you know what a witch could do with this? Just a touch of black magic, one quick chant, and your little half-breed would've dropped dead!"

Mom takes the shirt, shaking her head. "You're right. I've been so isolated by the magical community… I wasn't thinking." She sits beside Gwenna, her head bowed.

"You're all fools!" Gwenna continues, gesturing towards me. "That's the third time I saved your clueless daughter this week!"

"The third time?" I almost stutter. I want to pinch myself. I must be having a nightmare. How the hell did a bird turn into Aunt Gwenna?

"Yes, you moron! The first time was at your softball game. Did you not see me? I almost took your head off!"

"I didn't know that was you! I had no idea that you…" I can't even find the words. You're a bird? It sounds absurd.

"Oh, sweet Aurelia," Aunt Gwenna puts her hand on her chest. "Do your little spawns not even know that we're shape-shifters? Alaina, what have you been teaching them?"

"Shape-shifters?" Zoe sounds as confused as me.

"Of course! We're Crowes, you nimwit half-breeds!"

Mom stands, hands on her hips. "You're not going to speak to my daughters that way."

"We're crows," I repeat. I think back to all the times that I wandered the woods, my bird journal in hand, the pages soft and creased from constant use. I used to climb trees, all the way to the top, Logan on the ground, staring up at me, awe and fear etched on his face. I'd perch upon the highest branches, arms stretched out, a strong feeling in my gut that if I took the leap, I'd fly away to a better place. Birds landed on my arms, singing before they launched back into the sky, as if they somehow sensed that I was one of them. "Mom, how come you never told me? You never taught me how." Anger rises with my voice. I feel betrayed, cheated.

"It isn't that simple." Mom's head hangs down. "I can't shape-shift anymore. It's part of my punishment. They put a hex on me and my offspring. We'll never fly together with the crows." Her voice breaks. "I thought it was better if you never knew. I told myself that you couldn't miss what you never had. But then, there were times that I saw you, Saria," Mom's eyes turn glassy. "I saw you in the trees, and I knew that part of you knew what you are. What I took away from you."

"You didn't take anything from me." I point at Aunt Gwenna. "She did."

Aunt Gwenna holds up her hands. "It wasn't my decision. There was a vote. There was nothing I could do to stop it."

"I bet you tried really hard." I can't help the bitterness in my voice.

"This is the thanks I get for saving your butt THREE times?"

I put my hands on my hips. "What exactly did you save me from? And when?"

Aunt Gwenna puts up one finger. "Number one: the softball game. A witch was messing with you, making you all discombobulated. I swooped down and broke their spell."

"A witch?" I think back to that night, and the few days before: feeling hazy, seeing double, having trouble orienting myself. There were moments I thought I was losing my mind. Was it always a witch setting spells on me? "Who?" I ask.

"There were too many people nearby. I tried, but I couldn't hone in on the culprit."

I remember Mallory in the stands, a devilish grin on her face. "Mallory," I say. Even Giselle's been acting strange since Mallory moved to town. I wonder if she's bewitched her too.

Aunt Gwenna holds up two fingers. "Number two: I saved you in the woods. A group of Talon's witches created a flash storm. They would've finished you off if it wasn't for me." She holds up the bloody shirt, accentuating her point. "It wasn't an ordinary storm. It was a terror attack."

I clutch the crystal pendant around my neck. My stomach lurches. "I need to sit down." I lower myself into an armchair, my head in my hands. "It's real. They're after me."

"Number three: you idiots left this in the garbage, for anyone's taking!" Aunt Gwenna twirls the bloody shirt in the air. "Do you know how quick your life would've been over if this got in the wrong hands?"

"I didn't know," I say. My insides quiver, my bones rattling inside my skin.

"Enough!" Mom takes the bloody garment, throws it in a drawer, and slams it shut. "It's my fault. I saw her throw it away. I should've stopped her. Thank you, Gwenna, for returning it to us before something terrible happened." Mom pauses. "And for saving Saria."

"Three times," Aunt Gwenna hold up three fingers for emphasis. "In ONE week. You're lucky I flew by at the right times! I can't hover around twenty-four seven. You ladies need to get it together!"

"I set a protection spell on our home." Mom says.

Aunt Gwenna rolls her eyes. "You're out of practice, Alaina. Your protection spell is a joke. Might as well put a piece of duct tape on an unlocked door." She sighs. "Don't worry. I tightened up the security spells around here. It'll slow them down, but it won't prevent them from getting in. There's no spell that can hold up against that amount of power."

"Maybe if you'd allowed us in your schools, we'd have the skills to protect ourselves," Zoe says.

Her comment surprises me. Zoe never showed any interest in attending Enchantments Academy before. The summer before high school, I kept hoping that my letter of acceptance would show up in the mail, that they'd have a change of heart. When it never arrived, I moped for days. Zoe just shrugged, and disappeared into her room to practice guitar.

"What else can we do?" Mom asks.

"You can start by transferring some power to that one," Aunt Gwenna points to my sister.

"My name's Zoeli," Zoe says, even though we both know she knows that. I guess us half-breeds aren't worthy of being identified by name.

"She's a sitting duck," my aunt continues. "She could use a boost during this time." She faces me. "How about you sacrifice some of your precious powers for your pathetic sister? I've been watching you for a few days, and Lord knows you haven't been using your gift for noble purposes." She faces my mom. "A little humbling wouldn't hurt this one."

"Transfer?" I ask.

"Yes, you can transfer some of your power to your weakling sister. Alaina, have you taught them nothing?"

"I never thought a power transfer was necessary, but I suppose you're right," Mom says.

"Um, but," I start. "They're after ME. I need my powers to protect myself."

"They're after that one too," Gwenna points at my twin. "And she's utterly useless."

My heartbeat quickens. "But, but…" My powers are everything. They're all I have. As much as I hate them, I need them. Zoeli has friends and hobbies and passions that don't involve magic. She's an entire person. I wish I could be, but I'm not. My whole identity depends on my magic. "There has to be another way."

Zoe shakes her head, her lip curled in disgust. "She'd rather watch me die than give up one iota of her power."

Aunt Gwenna smirks. "Like mother, like daughter, they say."

Mom narrows her eyes. "And what's that supposed to mean?"

"You only thought of yourself when you married that human vermin. I was next in line to be queen, but you ruined that for me."

"I can't help who I fell in love with."

"You knew how much being queen meant to me." Aunt Gwenna spits out the words. "Lucky for all of you, I'm feeling a bit less bitter. I think I've found a way back to the throne." Her lips curl into a devious grin. "Or the castle, at least."

Mom's mouth makes an 'o' shape. "How?" She holds up her hand. "On second thought, I don't want to know. One thing I don't miss is all of the politics and scheming. Keep me out of it."

My aunt lifts her chin. "Gladly." With a cackle and an explosion of feathers, Aunt Gwenna soars out the open window. Her caws echo through the night sky, her wings fluttering as she sails across the full moon.

Chapter Nine

Zoeli

It's midnight, but I can't fall asleep. My mind keeps replaying the events of today: Damian walking me home, his tales of powerful creatures, witches becoming vampires, feeling powerless but pretending to be brave with enemies on our tail, Aunt Gwenna as a crow, smashing her beak into our house, and earlier, the note in my locker.

I jolt up in bed, and flick on my bedside lamp. I rummage through my backpack, and find the torn piece from a spell book. Who put this in my locker? Damian? That doesn't make any sense. If he wanted me to take Saria's powers, he could just tell me how. Who else knows? A shiver runs down my spine.

You don't have to be the weaker sister

Aunt Gwenna's voice echoes in my mind, "She's a sitting duck," "utterly useless." Tears pool in my eyes as I remember Saria's response. "There has to be another way," she said. One tear slips out. I wipe it away.

Since witches will strongly resist the removal of their powers, the success of this spell depends on: the strength of the witch conducting the evulsion, the phase of the moon, and the amount of blood and hair used. Even a powerful witch under a full moon is not likely to evulse more than ten percent of another witch's powers.

I cross my bedroom and swipe the curtains aside. Outside, the full moon beams, casting a glow over me. The larger the moon, the stronger the evulsion.

Could I really do that to my sister? It's immoral, not to mention illegal. But…given the dire circumstances, and Saria's resistance to helping her own twin sister, could my actions be justified? Even Aunt Gwenna said that she should transfer some power to me.

I skim the <u>*Warning!*</u> Since Saria and I are twins, we're most likely a match. Honestly, I doubt it will even work. It may be a full moon, but I'm no match for Saria. If the best-case scenario is ten percent of a witch's powers, I would be lucky to get five percent of Saria's, if I manage to get any at all. I don't think such a tiny amount of magic would cause a bad reaction.

I hold the yellowed page up in the moonlight.

<u>*Ingredients:*</u> *Blood of target witch, Hair of target witch, Three black candles*

In my mind's eye, I see Mom a few hours earlier, shoving the blood-covered shirt in a drawer. I'm going to do it. Saria has so much power that she won't even notice the difference, I tell myself. She has plenty to spare.

I push open my bedroom door. At the end of the hallway, a light shines from beneath Dad's office door. Who's up this late?

I tiptoe down the hall, and knock lightly on the office door. "Hello?"

There's no answer. I hear papers rustling, feet moving on the floor. "Hello?" I repeat.

The door swings open. I jump back, my hand on my chest.

"Zoeli?" Dad rubs his eyes.

"What're you doing up?" I ask, moving past him and into the office. His computer hums. Motherboards, wires, and other random computer parts are stacked alongside the monitor.

Dad sinks into his black leather office chair, his hands behind his head. "I must've fallen asleep at my desk. I'm working on an important project."

"Can you tell me about it?" I ask, leaning against his desk. "Or is it another top-secret project for the army?"

"It isn't a job," Dad says. "This is a personal project."

"Oh?" I raise my brows.

"Mom told me about what happened tonight," Dad says. "I'm working on a device that can detect the presence of witches and other supernatural creatures within a mile radius."

"Oh, wow," I say.

"The current record is held by a witch who could sense another witch's energy from two thousand feet. My device would more than double that."

I grin. "The pathetic human vermin can create magic that's more effective than the most powerful witches. Imagine that."

"Not magic," Dad says. "It's just technology."

I shrug. "Semantics."

"I need you to be safe," Dad says. "You, Saria and Mom. My family."

"We'll be okay, Dad." I wish I felt as certain as I sound. Fake it until you make it has always been my mantra. How much longer will I have to fake it?

Dad yawns. "I should head to bed. You too, Zoe. It's a school night."

"Goodnight, Dad," I say.

"Night, Zoe." Dad ruffles my hair.

I pretend to walk away. As soon as I hear his bedroom door shut, I slip inside the bathroom I share with my sister. As usual, the shower drain is packed with long blonde hair. I shove a clump in my pocket.

I tiptoe down the steps, peering over my shoulder every time the old floorboards creak beneath my feet. My breath comes faster as I move through the kitchen and down the hall. Inside the magic room, I close the door behind me. It clicks shut. The air is still. In the quiet, my heart pounds like a drum. It's so loud that I'm sure it'll wake up the whole house.

Fumbling in the dark, my hands in front of me, I move through the blackness until I feel the stiff velvet. I pull the curtains apart, revealing the splintered glass: a design like spiderwebs created by the impact of Gwenna's beak. The full moon shines through the broken glass, illuminating the walls with light interrupted by dark, jagged lines.

The bloody shirt is still in the drawer where Mom left it. With it clenched in my fist, I hear Aunt Gwenna's voice in my thoughts, "You idiots! Do you know what a witch could do with this?"

They never imagined it would be me.

I sort through the drawer of candles, and find three black ones. I have everything I need. *What am I doing?*

My heart races as I reread the instructions. *I can't do this. It's wrong.*

Yet, my body moves as if on autopilot. I arrange the three black candles as the points of a triangle in the center of the floor. *I love my sister.*

I sit inside the triangle, spinning around to light each candle. *She betrayed me.*

The clump of hair and bloody shirt are on my lap. *She deserves this.*

I read from the spell book page.

> "I'm inside this triangle
> With the blood and hair of a witch
> The power that harbors within her
> Is now mine to take and switch"

For a few moments, nothing happens. *It didn't work.*

I start to feel strange: dizzy, my face warm and tingly. I yelp in pain as something pierces me in the torso, tearing my insides apart. I clutch my stomach, expecting to find an open wound, but the skin is still intact.

A burning sensation overtakes me, like molten lava shooting through my veins. It seeps deeper and deeper, flooding every cell in my body. *Too much.* But I don't know how to stop it. It flows in: so free, so quick.

I remember the warning about taking too much power. It's dangerous. It could even kill. I didn't take it seriously because I never imagined it was a possibility.

My muscles spasm, pain searing through me as I'm lifted off the ground. I open my mouth to scream, but nothing comes out. I'm still thrashing in space when everything goes black.

Chapter Ten

Saria

I'm asleep when I feel something pulling at the core of my power. A small amount of energy flows out, escaping my body.

If I'd been awake, I would've been terrified. My conscious mind would rather die than relinquish my powers. But my subconscious has its own ideas.

Underneath the glamour and popularity, I hate my life, my fake life, and fake friends. I hate wondering if anything I have is real. I long to find out who I am, who I truly am, without any magic.

My conscious and subconscious are always at odds: a dissonance that haunts me every day. When I'm sleeping, my subconscious wins because it doesn't have an opponent.

The invasive force steals another bit of my magic. Take it! Take it all! I don't want any of it! Instead of fighting the invasive force, my dream-self pushes the power out. Relief washes over me as I cleanse my soul of the poison. I expel the power from my body, unsatisfied until the very last drop is gone.

As soon as I wake, I know something's off. I drag myself out of bed, my movements sluggish. When I reach for my powers, I find nothing.

My heart bangs against my chest. The dream. It couldn't be real. I shake my head. It's impossible. My powers will be back soon, right?

Staring into a full-length mirror, I'm disgusted by my reflection. No matter how much I fluff it, my hair is limp. Acne mars my cheeks. I try again and again to access my magic to no avail. My breaths are coming faster now. Dizzy, I sit on my vanity stool, my head in my hands. I can't go to school looking like this.

Outside, a horn blares. I push my curtains aside. In the driver's seat of her SUV, Giselle looks as beautiful as ever. Mallory and Penny are in the backseat.

Mallory throws her head back and laughs. It's as if she knows, and she's laughing at me. A shiver runs down my spine. She had something to do with this.

I'm being paranoid again. Or am I? Aunt Gwenna said there was a witch casting spells on me at the game. I saw Mallory there, a gleeful grin pasted on her face as she watched me falter.

Then again, the stands were packed. It could've been anyone. I'll find out who did this to me. And when I do, I'll make them pay. There will be no mercy for the bitch who put this hex on me.

I straighten out my shoulders and flip my hair one last time. Here goes nothing. I've always wondered what would happen if I lost my magic. I guess today's the day I find out.

As I slide into the passenger seat, Giselle's brow furrows. "Are you okay?"

"I'm fine." I smile even though it hurts.

"You look awful," Mallory says from the backseat.

My throat closes and my eyes brim with tears. I'm embarrassed that I care so much about what she thinks. I want to say something, anything, back to her. I want to put her in her place, but my mind is blank. I'm terrified that I'll stammer and choke on my words.

"Shut up," Penny sticks up for me. "Is something wrong, Saria? You look like you didn't sleep well." She coils a strand of her red hair around her finger, her eyes wide with concern.

I swallow, grateful for a true friend. "I had bad dreams." Was it a dream? What's happening to me?

"I have the best blush in my purse," Penny says. "It'll liven you right up. We'll go to the bathroom as soon as we get to school."

"Thank you."

True to her word, Penny helps me apply makeup in the bathroom. The bell rings. I wince at my reflection. All of the concealer, mascara and blush in the world isn't going to fix this disaster.

Shoulders slumped, I head into the hallways. Rather than clearing the way, students bump and rustle me, bodies and backpacks shoving me through the crowd.

Chad waits at my locker. "Hey babe," he says. I smile at him, hoping he still thinks I'm pretty. There were so many times I yearned for the ability to turn my powers off, and now I'm desperate to turn them back on. As much as part of me wants to know what's real, the other part is petrified. What if no one likes the real me?

"Good morning." My voice quivers.

Chad leans in and kisses me. "I'm excited for your game tonight, babe."

Oh, no. The big softball game. Tonight. This hex better wear off before the game. We're playing the toughest team in the state. Without my powers, we don't stand a chance. To Chad, I feign confidence. "We're going to crush 'em."

"Of course you are." The bell rings. "Later, babe." Chad kisses me again before he walks towards his first period class. "Love you."

I let out the breath I've been holding. "Love you, too."

***

I'm not used to feeling invisible. In the hallways, boys that used to gawk pass by without a second glance. I'm craving the rush of dopamine their attention provides. I'm nothing more than a drug addict: a fiend for adoration. When it doesn't come, I feel my spirits crash. Desperation seeps into my bones, drowning me inside.

At lunch, Mallory flirts shamelessly with my boyfriend. "Hey, Chad, have you been working out?"

"Yeah." Chad flexes his biceps

"I've noticed. You look amazing." Mallory bats her lashes.

Keisha rolls her big brown eyes.

"Ugh, I have a ton of homework." Penny grumbles.

Penny's words jog my memory. I have three pages of math homework due next period. As if on cue, Jack Williams, a boy who's done homework for me since eighth grade walks by. "Jack!"

Jack spins around. He peers at me thoughtfully, as though he doesn't recognize me. He readjusts his glasses, as if that might help. "Saria?"

"Hey," I say, trying to sound sultry. "If you do my math homework, I'll let you sit next to me in class." It's an offer he's never refused.

Jack bursts out laughing. "Nah, I think I'll pass." He strides away.

"Wow, Saria, guess you've lost your touch." Mallory giggles.

Giselle doubles over, her hand on Mallory's shoulder. Soon, both of my so-called friends are hysterical, banging their fists on the table, tears in their eyes from laughing so hard.

I swallow back tears of humiliation. "I'm going to the library." As I walk away, no one follows. No one tries to stop me. No one cares.

My vision blurs. I struggle to see through my tears as I weave through tables in the library. "Hey, Saria." I blink, and Logan comes into focus. He's alone at a table, algebra homework on the table in front of him.

"Logan!" My lips curve up, my first genuine smile of the day. Then, my insecurity kicks in. What if Logan doesn't like the real me?

Logan smiles back, and my fears fade away. "What are you up to?"

I gesture to his homework. "About to tackle that. How's it going?"

Logan shakes his head. "Not great, but two heads are better than one." He pats on the seat next to him. "We'll figure it out together."

I collapse into the chair next to him, my tension releasing, each muscle relaxing, one by one. After twenty minutes, our homework is complete. I stare in disbelief. "We did it." At first glance, the worksheet seemed impossible. The numbers, letters and symbols looked like a code I could never decipher. Logan didn't know where to start. I figured out the first few steps. When I got stuck, Logan came through in the end.

Logan grins. "We make a good team."

Team. The word echoes in my mind, and my smile falters.

"What's wrong?" Logan asks.

For a moment, I can't catch my breath. Did he notice how awful I look? "I-I-I know I look really bad today," I stammer. "I didn't sleep well."

A crease appears between Logan's brows. "What're you talking about? You look beautiful," he says.

I feel like my heart might explode. Warmth bursts from my center and shoots through my extremities. It almost feels like magic flowing through me. He still thinks I'm beautiful. Even without my magic. I can't believe it.

"But you seem upset," Logan continues. "Is everything okay?"

I shake my head. "When you said team, it reminded me that I have softball tonight." I suck in a deep breath. It shakes on its way out. "I'm worried that I'm not going to play well."

"Oh, because of what happened at the last game?" Logan asks. "You seemed a little off, but then you recovered."

"You were there?" I ask.

Logan nods. "I go to all of your games."

"Why didn't you say hi?" I say.

"You were busy with your friends." He rolls his pencil between his fingers. "I don't want to bother you."

"Logan!" I put my hand on top of his. Is that what he thinks? That he's a bother to me? "I don't ever want you to feel that way."

Staring at our hands, a smile touches his lips. "I'll make sure to say hi tonight."

"I'm not going to play well tonight." I twist a lock of hair around my fingers, smoothing the split ends. "I don't want to disappoint you." I put my head in my hands. Tears threaten to escape.

"Saria, what's going on? What's wrong?"

"People love me because I win," I say. "So, what will happen when I lose?"

"That's not why I love you." Logan holds out his hands and shakes his head. "As a friend, of course. I know you're taken and everything. And we've been friends forever."

I smile. "I know what you mean."

The bell rings. "See you later." I swing my backpack over my shoulder. As I'm walking away, fingers clamp around my shoulder. I spin around. Logan pulls me to him. His arms envelope me: my head feels fuzzy, my breath hitches in my throat. As we separate, he leans in, his lips brushing my forehead.

"Later, Saria." He grins as he turns away.

The center of my forehead tingles where he kissed me. It reminds me of the feeling when magic boiled in my gut: hot, exhilarating, euphoric. It spreads outwards: prickling my scalp and then gliding down my face: cheeks, burning, lips curving into a smile, heat spiraling down my spine.

His kiss is like magic.

Chapter Eleven

Zoeli

Voices reverberate from above. "I didn't know that one had it in her!" Aunt Gwenna sounds like she's a million miles away. Her voice echoes like it's traveling through a long tunnel. I don't know where I am, but it's unbearably hot. It's as if I stripped and sprawled out across the sun, my naked skin blistering on its molten plasma. "Not only did she manage to pull off an evulsion, she stole from her own sister. Guts and vengeance. I like it!" Maybe I'm burning in hell. There has to be consequences for what I did. I just didn't imagine they'd come so quickly.

"Stop blabbering, Gwenna. I need help. My daughter's not well!"

"In a few hours, she'll be feeling better than ever." Gwenna cackles.

"If she survives," Mom says. A hand presses on my forehead. "She's burning up. I can't do this alone."

"Okay, okay," Aunt Gwenna grumbles. "But for the record, this is the fourth time I'm saving one of your nimwit half-breeds this week."

"Noted. Now get to work." Cold crystals run up and down my arms, across my forehead, and down my nose. My mom and aunt chant under their breaths, a language I don't know but somehow understand. They ask the elements for healing. They call on Mother Earth to repair my failing organs.

I feel waves washing over me, cool, refreshing, invigorating from head to toe. My eyes flutter open. Mom and Aunt Gwenna are blurry forms, looming over me, their silhouettes black against the glowing light around them. I suck in a deep breath, pulling the glowing energy into my lungs. It moves inside me, renewing every cell as it rushes through.

The world comes into focus. Aunt Gwenna smirks, one eyebrow raised high as though she's amused. Mom, on the other hand, looks mad as hell.

Smack! I jolt upright, my hand protecting my stinging cheek. "You hit me." It's the first time Mom ever put her hands on me. The shock and disbelief that she could do that hurts so much more than the slap.

"You idiot!" Mom shouts. "What were you thinking? How could you do this to your sister?"

Suddenly, I'm furious. "I had no choice. Saria would rather watch me die than give up a speck of her power." I point to my aunt. "Even Aunt Gwenna said that I was a sitting duck. Am I right?"

"Don't forget useless and weakling."

When I glare at my aunt, power bursts out of me. Like a dam breaking, I can't control it. Thud! Aunt Gwenna launches into the air and slams into the wall. A dozen crystals avalanche off a shelf and clatter onto the floor.

"Holy crap!" My hand clamps over my mouth. "I'm sorry! Are you okay?"

Aunt Gwenna stands up and straightens her hair. "Oh, I'm fine." She waves her hand. "I've been dealt much harder blows from much more powerful witches." She shrugs. "But it's not a bad start if you find yourself up against Talon or any of his crew."

I smile. It's the first semi-compliment that Aunt Gwenna has ever given me, so I'll take it. "Not so fast," Mom says. "You're not keeping Saria's powers. When she gets home from school, you're going to apologize and give them back."

I fold my arms across my chest. "She wouldn't do it for me."

"She's not wrong," Aunt Gwenna muses. I never thought I'd say this, but Aunt Gwenna is earning some major points in my book.

"What are you saying, Gwenna?" Mom says. "Allow her to break magical law and steal from her own sister?"

"All I'm saying is that she's always been the weaker sister. I don't see any harm in letting her have a little fun."

You don't have to be the weaker sister. Did Aunt Gwenna put that note in my locker? But why? Something tells me that she can't be trusted. There's another agenda; something bigger going on here.

"For how long?" Mom asks.

"I don't know, Alaina. Since I didn't breed with a human vermin, my daughter doesn't have this problem."

I look past my mom, through the open door and into the empty hallway. It suddenly occurs to me that Saria might not be okay. Why isn't she barging through the door and demanding her powers back herself? "Where is she?"

"At school."

I turn to the clock hanging on the wall, and my mouth drops open. It's almost two o'clock. I missed the whole day.

Saria went to school… Without her powers… I wonder how that's going.

Chapter Twelve

Saria

"How's it going?"

"Never been better." I can't help the sarcasm in my tone as I pinch myself again. Please let me wake up from this nightmare. God, I'll do anything. Just please, please, let me wake up.

"What's your problem?" Giselle stares at the purple blotch of skin crushed between my fingers.

"I'm just… not myself today." The irony isn't lost on me. This is the first day I've ever been my true self.

"I'm sorry about before. We were just joking around."

I shrug.

"Snap out of it!" Giselle snaps her fingers in front of my face. "It's game time."

"I can't play."

"This is an important game. We need you." Giselle grabs my arm and pulls me towards the doors.

As I trot towards the field, I decide that I'll just play the best I can. I can't be that bad at softball. Right?

"Hey, Keisha," I say. "Let's warm up."

Keisha raises her eyebrows. "You're serious?"

"Yeah, sure," I say, trying to sound casual.

Keisha's brow furrows, but then she shrugs and squats at home plate. I practice rotating my arm around like a windmill. I got this. I've done this thousands of times before. As my arm circles, the ball feels heavier than I remember. I release way too late. The pitch flies over Keisha's head.

"Sorry!" My cheeks redden as Keisha runs to retrieve the ball.

My next few pitches are just as wild. Keisha trots up to the pitcher's mound. "Everything okay?" she whispers.

I bite my lip, fighting back tears. "Batter up!" The umpire pulls a mask over his face. Black metal covers his features, only his eyes visible. They bore into mine, changing colors and shapes: human to animal, animal to demon, blue to glowing red irises, surrounding jet black pupils.

I gasp and drop my gaze. Keisha puts her hand on my shoulder. "You got this, Sar! Get your head in the game." One pat on my back and she jogs away.

"Play ball!" The umpire says. When I raise my chin, the umpire's eyes are blue again. What's wrong with me? Is someone messing with me? I scan the faces in the crowd. Have I finally lost my mind?

"Saria! Saria! Saria!" Fans chant my name. In the bleachers, bodies blur together until their arms are dozens of tentacles attached to one massive octopus-like creature. It watches me with hundreds of eyes.

I raise my chin to the sky and whisper. "Whatever I did to deserve this, I'm sorry. I've learned my lesson. Please, please, I need my powers."

My first pitch bounces in front of the plate. "Ball one."

Instead of worrying about speed, I focus on throwing in the strike zone. I lob the next pitch right down the center. The batter drives the ball into the outfield. In center field, Giselle's eyes pop open in surprise as the ball sails past her. She does a double take before turning around and chasing the ball.

The batter runs to third base. Tears burn in the corners of my eyes. It's the first time I've given up a hit all season.

"It's okay, Saria!" Giselle shouts, throwing the ball in. The next batter jogs to the plate. She knocks dirt off her cleats. My arms shake violently. The ball almost slips out of my hand. *I can't do this.*

"You got this, Saria!" Logan stands in the crowd. When I look over, he smiles. I can't help but smile back. *I can do this.*

I windmill and then release the ball. "Ball one." Okay, I'll get this next pitch. "Ball two." I grit my teeth and try again. "Ball three." I can barely see through the tears that well up in my eyes. "Ball four." The batter takes first base.

My head is swimming. I can't breathe. It's like I'm underwater, drowning, the world floating around me.

The hair on the nape of my neck stands up, chills jolting down my spine. I'm shivering so hard that my whole body convulses. I can't shake the uncanny feeling that someone's watching me.

Staring at the full bleachers, I almost slap myself on the forehead. Of course someone's watching me. Dozens of my classmates are gawking, their mouths hanging open in disbelief.

I wish I had the power to disappear. But the truth is, the old Saria already has.

A wave of nausea rushes over me. Unsteady on my feet, I crouch on the ground, my head in my hands. I'm not sure how long I'm like that, but it feels like a hundred years.

Shadows surround me, blocking out the last glimmers of sunlight. "Are you okay?" I hear Keisha's voice. The shadows close in, their black forms enveloping me.

Giselle kneels beside me. "What's wrong, Saria?" I lift my chin. Giselle's eyes are wide, worry lines etched across her forehead. But is it real? Can I trust her?

"Back up! Everybody back up!" Coach Nelson jogs up, and my teammates step back.

"Saria? Are you okay?"

"I-I-I'm not feeling well." I stutter. "I'm dizzy." It's a half-truth, but it isn't a lie.

Coach helps me stand. I lean against her shoulder. "Let's go sit down. Giselle, you take the mound."

Giselle's eyes light up. She's always wanted to pitch, but Coach never gave her a chance. *It's my fault.* I knew that she practiced for hundreds, maybe thousands of hours. I also knew that her mom spent a boatload on private lessons. *Here I am, wondering if she's a good friend to me, but never looking in the mirror.*

As I walk to the dugout, I see Mallory in the stands. She grins, her mouth wider than the Cheshire cat. When I scowl, she winks.

That bitch. I know she had something to do with this. All of it. I just have to figure out how. If only I could think clearly...

Coach Nelson guides me to the bench. My parents are on the other side of the chain-link fence. "We're taking you home," Mom says.

"She might need to see a doctor." Coach says.

Mom's lips are pressed together in a firm line. I never told her that I depend on my powers to win. Even though it's against magical law to use your powers for personal gain, most witches do it from time to time. If it's done infrequently, the magical court turns the other cheek. But… I doubt that anyone would grant a pardon on my behalf.

I don't think that Mom would turn me in. Even if she did, there's not a court-sanctioned consequence that could hurt me more than the disappointment etched all over her face. Now Mom knows the truth. I'm a failure and a fraud. Plus, I'm pretty sure that I'm grounded for the rest of eternity.

"When we get home, we're having a family meeting," Mom says. "There's a lot to discuss."

I drop my gaze to the ground. Not only is she going to berate me, but she wants Zoeli to bear witness to my persecution. Once they're done with me, I won't have a shred of dignity left.

"Pack up," Mom says. "And meet us in the parking lot."

Nearby, people whisper. "Saria looks awful."

"She's so overrated."

"What's wrong with her?"

I shake my head, willing it to stop. But that doesn't work anymore.

"Hey, are you okay?"

My head snaps up. Logan's fingers slide through the chain-link fence, curling around the silver metal. "I'm fine."

He studies me, his hazel eyes piercing mine. "Don't lie to me, Saria."

I glance over at the bleachers. Mallory leans towards Chad. She crosses and uncrosses her legs, her calf brushing against his as she talks animatedly. Then, they both burst out laughing. He didn't even walk over to ask if I'm alright.

I turn back to Logan. "You want to get out of here?" I ask.

He raises his brows. "For real?"

My parents will be furious, but I'm getting a verbal lashing either way, so why the hell not? I grab the top of the fence, pull myself up and swing my legs over. "Let's go." I break out into a run. "Can't catch me!" As I sprint across the grass, I hear Logan's breaths behind me. His footsteps come faster, and a hand taps me on the back.

"Got you!" Logan says, whizzing past me. I chase him, giddy with laughter. He spins around, moving side-to-side, taunting me. I lunge forward. He dives out of the way. My arm sails through thin air.

"I'll get you!" We're facing each other, both grinning wildly. Logan bounces on the balls of his feet like a boxer. I wait for the right moment. I pounce.

My body slams into his, knocking us both to the ground. I'm on top of him, our faces inches apart. "I win," I say.

"Are you sure about that?" He wraps his arms around me and turns over. I wriggle, but he's holding on tight. On top of me, he pins my arms to the ground. "Surrender!"

"Never!" I squirm, laughter escaping my throat. Out of the corner of my eye, I see Mom. She's pacing in front of her car. She looks down at her watch. "We have to go," I whisper. "I'm sneaking away." I tilt my head towards my mom. She hasn't noticed me yet.

Logan's gaze follows my gesture. As soon as he's distracted, I push and roll out from underneath him. I jump to my feet. "I win," I whisper.

"Hey!" Logan charges towards me.

"Shhh!" I hold my finger to my lips, ducking behind a car.

Logan crouches beside me. "Why are we hiding?"

"Mom wants me to come home." I drop my gaze to the ground. "I can't face them yet. They're waiting for me, but I want to disappear with you."

"I can't do that to your mom. She'll be worried sick."

"I know," I grumble. I stand up and dust off my pants. "I guess I'll see you."

"Hold on." Logan grabs my hand. "I didn't say that you should go." His thumb runs across my palm, and sparks race down my spine. "Let me handle this," he says. "Wait here." Logan trots across the parking lot, waving to my parents. When they see him, they smile.

I can't hear what they're saying, but a few minutes later, my parents get into their car and drive away. Logan jogs back to me, a triumphant smile lighting up his face.

"How did you do it?"

"Magic." Logan grins. If he only knew…

I slide into the passenger seat of Logan's sedan. The seats are soft and worn, fraying at the edges. It's nothing like Chad's brand-new luxury leather. But I'd rather be here.

A few minutes later, we pull into Logan's driveway. His house is surrounded by woods that I know by heart. I've trekked through them so many times, navigating my way from my backyard to his. I close my eyes, remembering the sequence of textures as though they're beneath my feet: a worn dusty path leading to a thick, patchy mud, the ground always damp from the stream trickling through, bumpy tree roots emerging from below, pointing the way through the thicket and to the light shining from Logan's house.

My eyes fly open. "The treehouse! Is it still there?"

Logan shuts off the engine. "Of course. I'd never take it down."

"I'll race you there!" I'm out of his car and jetting across the lawn. I'm not using magic, so it's harder than it used to be. My chest heaves and my breath sputters.

I'm moving so fast I almost slam into the tree. I grab a rung and hoist myself up, climbing up the wooden boards until I'm in the treehouse. Logan is right behind me.

"I win!" I say.

"Not fair!" Logan crosses his arms across his chest. "You had a head start!" It feels like deja vu, except for Logan's much taller now. His head brushes against the ceiling.

I stand against the wall, memories rushing through me. Our dads, hauling the lumber, saw and power drills. Logan and I drilling in the boards, my cheeks shaking from smiling so wide. Sitting up here for hours, bird watching, talking and joking, our feet swinging over the ledge.

My fingers trace the letters etched into the wall.

Logan + Saria = Best Friends Forever

I remember chiseling them out myself, the friction from the carving knife callusing my hand. "I'm a bad friend," I say.

"Why do you say that?"

"I haven't treated you well these past few years."

Logan shrugs. "People drift apart. It happens." He acts like it's no big deal but I see the hurt flash in his eyes.

"And not just to you, either," I say, thinking of the way I stole the spotlight from Giselle, knowing how bad she wanted to pitch. "I want to start hanging out with you more again. Like old times."

Logan's lips press into a firm line. "Chad won't like that."

He's right. Before I started dating Chad, Logan and I had already started drifting apart. Once Chad and I got serious, he didn't like me hanging out with other guys, even if I promised it was platonic.

"Maybe I don't care what Chad says anymore." I'm not sure why I ever did. I was chasing an image: Ken and Barbie, prom king and queen, the high school dream couple. In order to be the perfect girl, I needed the perfect boyfriend. I thought that perfection would make me feel complete. It didn't. The outside facade only amplified the emptiness inside, the hollowness behind my smile. "Maybe Chad won't be in the picture for much longer."

"Really?" Logan raises his eyebrows, the corner of his lip curving into a half-smile. A dimple materializes on his cheek.

"Let's go to the top," I say.

"But…"

Before Logan can finish his sentence, I'm climbing up the bark, grasping branches and lifting myself up, up, up, until I reach the highest point. I perch on the bough and spread my arms wide, wind whistling through my fingers.

"You're insane." Logan watches me from below, eyes wide.

Laughter erupts from my throat: a wild, chaotic sound that I barely recognize as my own. "I might be," I say. "Come on up." I pat the space beside me.

Logan pulls himself up, cheeks bright red, a vein bulging in his forehead. He wobbles on his knees as he makes his way to me. "Wow." Logan says, sliding next to me. "Absolutely beautiful." He's looking at me, but I think he's talking about the view.

"Up here, I'm far away from everything and everyone. I can finally have a moment of peace."

"But you're not far away from me."

"That's even better," I pause, considering. "I'm even more at peace with you."

"I'm glad that I can do that for you," Logan says. "But when you find true peace within yourself, nothing can disrupt that." As the sun descends, Logan's eyes match the dusky sky.

"You're right." Our legs touch, and warmth spreads through me. When did Logan start having this effect on me? "On the inside, I'm at war between who I really am and who everyone thinks I am." I sigh. "And I'm not even sure that I can tell the difference anymore." I shake my head. "From the first time I pitched a no hitter, the applause was intoxicating. It became an addiction." I'm overcome by the urge to tell Logan everything. Magical law prohibits witches from telling humans about our abilities, but it's not like I haven't already broken almost every law in the book anyway. If I never share the truth of who I am with anyone, I'll always feel alone. I want Logan to know all of me: the real me, whoever that is. "Logan, I'm going to tell you something that I've never told anyone before." My voice shakes.

Logan's expression darkens. "What's going on?"

I take a deep breath and blurt out, "I'm a witch."

Logan's eyes widen and then he bursts into laughter. Does he think I'm joking? Tears sting the corners of my eyes. No one will ever understand me. Logan shakes his head. "I'm sorry. I'm not laughing at you. I'm relieved. I thought someone was hurting you." Logan puts his arm around me. His eyes meet mine. "Saria, I've known that for years."

"What?" My jaw drops open.

"Now I have a confession to make." Logan looks down. "When we were kids, I asked you what was in that room at the end of the hallway. The room that was always locked." He pauses. "I can tell when you're lying. You stiffen up, scrunch your nose and look to the left. You told me that we're not allowed in there because it's under construction. Do you remember that?"

I shrug. "I think so."

"A few nights later, we were watching a movie, and when I said I was going to the bathroom..." His voice trails off.

"What did you do?"

"I picked the lock." Logan wrings his hands. "I'm sorry. I saw all of it: shelves full of books about witchcraft, candles, crystals, jars with herbs and potions."

"You little sneak!"

"I learned from the best. Wasn't it you who showed me how to break into Ms. Cooper's garden?"

"Touche." I grin. "But I only wanted one pink tulip. You didn't have to keep going back."

"They're your favorite." Logan leans closer. His face is almost touching mine. Electricity courses through me. "I would've kept going back every day, forever–"

"If Ms. Cooper's dog didn't almost kill you." I finish his sentence.

Logan rolls up his sleeve, revealing a series of scars shaped like a rottweiler's teeth. "Yeah, that bastard got me good." He smiles, dimples indenting his cheeks. "But I still got you that pink tulip."

"You did." I shake my head, remembering Logan trotting up my porch, a pink tulip in his hand, his arm soaked in blood. I wanted to heal him so badly, but I thought that I couldn't share my secret. Meanwhile, he knew all along. "And a trip to the ER."

Logan shrugs. "I'd do it again." A gust of wind shakes the tree. I wrap my arms around Logan, remembering what happened last time I was in the woods. What if this tree collapses right now? In my mind's eye, I see us sprawled out on the ground, our necks broken. Coming up here was really stupid. "I'm worried about you, Saria. I want to be there for you. Tell me what's bothering you so much."

"Everything." I pause. "I woke up this morning, and my powers are gone. They're just *gone*. Without them, I'm a total loser. I can't even play softball." My voice breaks.

"That doesn't make you a loser in my book." Logan says. "I don't care about how well you play softball. You're still amazing to me."

"Maybe to you, but not to everyone else." I drop my gaze to the ground. A squirrel darts across the ground. From way up here, with my feet swaying, it looks like I could squash it like a bug. It's funny how perspective distorts things. "When I don't perform, I see the disappointment in their eyes, and it kills me. They expect me to be perfect, but I'm not. Without my magic, I'm a loser." Tears blur my vision. "I'm a total joke."

"Don't talk about yourself that way." Logan puts his hand under my chin and lifts it up. Our eyes meet. "I think the problem here isn't what they think of you, but what you think of yourself."

"I don't even know what to think of myself," I say. "I've used magic as a crutch for so long. I don't even know what I'm capable of without it."

"Maybe this is a blessing in disguise. This could be the best thing that ever happened to you."

"Or the worst."

"This is an opportunity for you to grow. Embrace it. I believe that everything happens for a reason," Logan says. "I think this will make you stronger than you ever were."

"I hope you're right." A small brown bird perches on the end of a long, craggy branch. I study it, my brow furrowing. It seems to stare at me, and then it takes off, fluttering across the orange-streaked sky. "That looks like a nightingale," I murmur. "But that doesn't make any sense."

"Why not?" Logan asks.

"Because nightingales are from Europe, Asia and Africa. They don't live on this side of the world." I shake my head. "I must be seeing things."

Or maybe it wasn't a bird after all… I think of Aunt Gwenna, the burst of black feathers, her human body morphing into a crow. Are other shape-shifters lurking around here? If so, what do they want? Fear crawls under my skin, squeezing my heart. I shudder.

"Are you cold?" Logan wraps his arms around me. I lean into his warmth, savoring it for one moment before I remember that we could be in danger. An owl hoots, as if in warning.

"We should get out of here," I say.

Logan checks his watch. "You're right. I promised your mom I'd have you home by eight." I climb down the branches, Logan following close behind. "If your mom asks, we finished part one of our science project."

My feet touch the ground. "Part one?"

Logan lands, not nearly as gracefully as me. He stumbles, and I put my arms around his waist to steady him. We're both breathing heavily, but I can't tell if it's from exertion or how close we're standing. My heart beats fast, a frantic flurry of warmth and nerves. Chad never made me feel like this. Our bodies are pressed together, our breaths shaky. "Yeah, the part that's due tomorrow." Logan grins. "You know, if we didn't finish it tonight, we'd fail for the year."

I smile. "You little sneak. I thought you said that you couldn't lie to my mom."

"I didn't say that I wouldn't lie to her. I said that I didn't want to worry her." Logan touches my hair, tentatively, his finger twirling around the ends. "But there isn't much I wouldn't do for you. I hope that I cheered you up, at least a little bit."

"More than a little bit," I breathe. His lips are so close to mine. Electricity pulses between us.

My phone rings, and the magic is broken. I slide my phone out of my pocket. "It's Chad," I say.

Logan pulls away from me, and it's like all the warmth in the world has been stolen away. I shiver. Head down, sandy-blonde hair covering his hazel eyes, Logan walks away. "I'll meet you at my car." His shadow follows him down the trail, growing longer as the sunlight wanes. Hands in his pockets, he kicks rocks out of the way.

Chapter Thirteen

Zoeli

My fingers strum my guitar with ease that I never imagined. Yaz's voice fills Scott's garage, belting out the lyrics of "Unspoken Regret."

"I could have just apologized
Instead I conceal the hurt
Underneath a cloak of resentment
Every day I put on my disguise
Pretend that I don't care
But if you look deep into my eyes
You'd find what's really there
Unspoken regret
is tearing me apart
Burns down in my core
Eats away at my heart
One day I won't have one anymore."

Eyes closed, I'm lost in the melody. I don't need to concentrate on the chords; my fingers move as if possessed by a master guitarist.

"Put my pride aside...
I'm down on my knees...
I know I'm not perfect
And I'll never be
But can you forgive me?"

Justin drops to his knees, playing his solo verse on his guitar. I can feel the magic inside me, bubbling in my core. I can't control it. Power pulses out of me, surging from my fingertips, filling the garage with magical energy.

The song ends. Justin jumps in the air. Yazmin's eyes are wide, "Wow," she breathes. Scott stands up at his drum set, his eyes glassy.

"That was amazing!" Scott walks over and swoops me up into a hug. My feet lift off the ground as he spins me around. I'm giddy, laughing wildly.

When he finally puts me down, he doesn't let go. Scott stares at me, his arms around my shoulders, a trance-like expression on his face. "Zoeli, you're so beautiful."

I pull myself out of his embrace. "Scott, stop being weird."

"You're the most incredible girl in the whole world."

I snap my fingers in front of his face. "Snap out of it. You're creeping me out."

"That was our most epic practice yet," Yazmin says. "Let's go out to celebrate."

"Club Ice?" Justin suggests. "My brother's friend works the door. I can get us in."

I'm not a good dancer. At the club, I spend most of my time swaying in the corner, invisible amongst all the sexy vixens who look like they were born to twerk. But tonight might be different. "Let's go!"

***

An hour later, we're inside Club Ice. We didn't need Justin's connection after all. One smile and a quick wink, and the security guard lifted the rope to let me and my friends enter. The entire world is at my fingertips. Before I even order a drink, I'm drunk off the power. It's exciting and terrifying all at once.

In the center of the dance floor, my hips move of their own volition, in perfect rhythm with the beat. Guys gather around, gawking, shoving each other out of the way, fighting for a chance to dance with me.

A hottie with blue eyes and huge biceps leans in. "You're gorgeous," he says. This guy is model material, and way out of my league. Yesterday, he wouldn't have noticed that I existed.

It should feel good, but it doesn't. It's phony, manufactured, based on a lie. For years, I envied Saria. I longed for the adulation she inspired. Now that it's mine, I don't even want it.

When Saria used to complain about all the attention, I rolled my eyes. I even accused her of being ungrateful. From the outside looking in, it's easy to make snap judgments about intentions and motivations. It's easy to get caught up in how things appear on the surface, and never imagine what's going on underneath. Assumptions are just that: assumptions. Maybe I was wrong about Saria.

The back of my neck prickles. A shiver works its way down my spine. Someone's watching me. When I turn around, Damian leans against the far wall, his angular face intermittently shrouded by shadows and then glowing as a strobe light flashes overhead. His lips twist into a scowl. What's that about?

I push my way through the crowd, sweaty bodies bumping and grinding, eyes ogling as I pass. "Hey!" I shout over the music.

Damian is mid-conversation with a guy who looks eerily like him. They share similar chiseled features and strong jawlines, but while Damian's eyes and hair are black, the guy he's talking to has ice blonde hair and silver eyes.

"Hey!" I yell louder, wondering if he didn't hear me. When he doesn't respond again, it's clear that he's ignoring me. "Hey!" I push his chest lightly.

He faces me, his eyes narrowed. "What do you want?"

I fold my arms across my chest. "What the hell's your problem?" I can't believe I actually thought that we were friends. I'm such an idiot.

"I would ask the same about you, but it's fairly obvious."

"What are you talking about?"

The guy beside Damian lifts his eyebrows, his silver eyes amused. "Are you going to introduce me to your friend, Damian?"

"Introduce yourself," Damian says.

"Colson Nightingale." He extends his hand. "Damian's cousin." I see it then, on his bicep. The crown. Colson's a royal, too.

"Zoeli McKinney-Crowe." I shake his hand.

Colson's eyes twinkle. "The notorious Crowe family. Tales of your mother's bravery travel far and wide."

"And stupidity," Damian says.

"Why's she stupid?" I ask, hands on my hips. "For falling in love with a human?"

"I've dated humans," Colson curls his lip, revealing a mouthful of shark-like teeth, white and gleaming. "They're fun. Subservient. Easy to manipulate. If you're into that kinda thing." Colson's salacious grin tells me that he *is* into that kinda thing.

"But you wouldn't marry one!" Damian scoffs, as though it's the most preposterous idea in the world.

"No, of course not," Colson admits. "But I admire Alaina Crowe's willingness to go against the grain."

"You're both disgusting." The words fly out of my mouth with such venom that spit sprays into the air, glistening in the blinking lights.

"Hypocrite," Damian's voice is full of disdain. "You're the last person who should preach ethical treatment of humans. What makes it even worse is that your father's one."

"What are you talking about?" I shake my head. "I haven't done anything wrong."

"Oh, really?" Damian uses his chin to gesture at a boy standing on my left. The stranger stares at me as if he's in a trance, his mouth wide-open, drool dripping down his chin. "Enrapturing half of this club with your thrall, taking away their free will, forcing them to behave in a humiliating manner. Shall I go on? Your actions are not only inhumane, but also illegal, if I choose to report you to the royal court."

"You think I'm doing this on purpose? Why would I do that?"

Damian shrugs. "You tell me. Some twisted need to feel powerful. Maybe it's a kink for you: your own personal slave that will do everything and anything you ask, a toy to play with and control."

"I can't believe that you think that lowly of me."

"I believe what my eyes tell me." Damian points to the throng of guys lingering nearby. When I glance their way, they share the same goofy grin.

"Do you think I'm enjoying this?" I shout. "I can't help it!"

"Sweetheart, I wasn't born yesterday. You may be able to fool those pathetic human vermin, but not me, baby."

"I can't control it," I repeat. "I'm not lying."

"I've been watching you for weeks," Damian hisses. "You had perfect control until tonight." Damian shakes his head. "I misjudged you. I thought you were sweet and goodhearted…" His voice trails off. "I didn't even realize how powerful you are. So, I guess you fooled me, too."

"Damian–" He raises his hand and my tongue catches in my throat. It's a tactic to let me know that he's still more powerful than me.

"I don't want to hear it." He waves his hand, dismissing me, and turns around. I stare at his broad back, muscles rippling underneath his black t-shirt. Fists clenched at my sides, I stomp away, blinking fast to stop my tears from spilling over.

Damian hates me. Why do I even care? I hate him, too: his overinflated ego, his stupid arrogant smirk, and his prejudiced jackass cousin, too. And why has he been watching me for *weeks?* He's nothing but a creepy stalker. I'm glad to be rid of him.

Across the room, Yazmin and Justin dance, their arms wrapped around each other. Justin whispers something in her ear, and Yazmin bursts out laughing. Sometimes I wish I could find a love like that. But I'm fine on my own. Really, I am.

"I bought you a drink." Scott shoves a drink in front of me, his movements fast and jerky, soda splashing out of the cup and onto my dress. "I'm so sorry." Scott's mouth opens in horror. "Zoe, are you okay?"

I grab the drink from his hand. "I'm fine. I don't melt when wet. I'm not the Wicked Witch of the West." Or am I? Here I am, bewitching my own friend. Scott looks like a puppy dog salivating over a piece of meat. It makes me feel gross.

I want to pretend that Damian doesn't exist, but I can't help it. My gaze drifts over to him. The most beautiful woman that I've ever seen moves towards Damian with an otherworldly grace, her pale skin glistening, flawless, almost ethereal. Platinum-blonde waves cascade down her back, all the way to the waistband of her form-fitting jeans. She stands next to Damian, her lean body brushing against his. I feel sick.

"Did it hurt?" A stranger leans in too close. His garlic breath makes me want to gag.

My brow furrows. "Excuse me?"

"When you fell from heaven, because you look like an angel." It's the lamest pickup line I've ever heard.

I need to get out of here. I glance over at my friends. Justin and Yazmin are still laughing, their hands in the air as they bounce to the music. There's no reason for me to ruin their night. I'll take an uber home.

I push my way through the crowd, elbowing a few gropers out of the way. The exit door slams shut behind me. As

I suck in the crisp night air, my heart rate slows. I inhale deeply, filling my belly up with oxygen.

I want to go to bed and pretend this night never happened. I slip my phone out of my purse and open the Uber App. No service. That's odd. I head into the parking lot, holding my phone out in front of me. I'm in a dead zone.

I walk further, waiting for the bars that indicate signal strength to appear on my screen. I keep going, my gaze glued to my phone, lost in my thoughts. Damian's voice replays in my mind: the clipped tone, full of contempt. I wonder if he'll report me to the royal court. They'd love any excuse to throw a nimwit half-breed in the dungeon and throw away the key.

When I finally look up, I'm all alone. The laughter and music from the club is gone. My footsteps echo in the silence. The road is deserted: not a house in sight. I frantically press buttons on my phone, willing it to work.

A wolf emoji appears on my screen. What the hell is going on? The wolf bares its teeth. Has Verizon gone bonkers? The emoji wolf snarls, and I jump, my phone clattering on the pavement. The screen cracks, glass splintering like a spiderweb, or a gunshot.

The wind whistles, a loud cackle reverberating through the trees. My blood runs cold. I'm not alone. The emoji wolf isn't an iPhone malfunction. I'm under attack.

The bushes part, and a white wolf emerges. I freeze, taking in her glowing yellow eyes, shiny fur, and long, powerful frame. A savage beast, but breathtakingly beautiful at the same time. She leans back on her haunches, tail swishing behind her. A low growl emits from her throat.

I have a split second to decide between flight or fight. It's more than likely that I'm dead either way. Since I was never much of a runner, I choose to fight. I thrust my arms forward, remembering what I did earlier when I slammed Aunt Gwenna into the wall. Power surges from my fingertips, sailing straight towards the wolf.

It doesn't even slow her down. She pounces, her muscular body flying through the air before she crashes into me. I propel backwards, my body slamming onto the road, the wolf hovering over me, her paws digging into my shoulder blades. She swipes me, her enormous claws cutting my dress open and slicing through my skin, but I barely register the pain.

"Get off of her." The voice comes from behind me. The wolf looks up. Damian steps beside me. "Licinia, I mean it. NOW."

Clouds of black smoke obscure the wolf, and when it clears, the beautiful woman from the club has taken its place. She pouts, hands on her hips. "I wanted a snack. What's it to you?"

"Get out of here, Licinia. If you know what's good for you." Damian points towards the woods.

"What're you going to do about it, Nightingale?" Licinia bares her teeth, revealing long white fangs. She saunters towards Damian, her silver-blonde hair swaying behind her.

"One snap of my fingers and the royal forces will be here." They're face to face now, their noses almost touching. "And that won't end well for you, Wolfe."

"You're no fun anymore, Damian," Licinia says. "And you chose the wrong side. Our militia's growing by the day. Pretty soon you and your royals will be answering to us...if we decide to let you live" She runs one finger down his chest. "I remember the good times we used to have, so maybe I'll have mercy on you."

"This is the last time I'm telling you, Licinia. Get out of here. NOW."

Licinia smirks. "Until we meet again, love." A haze of black smoke materializes and then dissipates. Licinia's gone. A bat soars into the sky and vanishes into the forest.

Damian sits on the ground next to me. "Are you okay?"

"I think so." I shake my head, trying to process everything. "I'm in shock more than anything."

"She scratched you up pretty good." Damian unzips his jacket and hands it to me.

I look down, realizing that half of my breasts are showing. Grateful, I wrap Damian's jacket around me, covering myself. It smells musky and masculine, like him. "So Licinia..." I wrinkle my brow. "Is she a wolf and a bat?"

"She's a wolf because she's a shifter. She's a bat because she's a vampire. All vampires are bats."

"She's the one you were telling me about..." My voice trails off. "The Wolfes were the original rulers of Aurelia. Licinia broke the law when she transitioned into a vampire. The Wolfes were removed from the throne, and the Crowes took over."

"You're a star student."

"That would make Licinia over a hundred years old."

"Looks pretty good for an old lady." Damian smirks. "Time passes, but she stays seventeen forever. That's how old she was when she changed over. She was sentenced to eternity in the dungeon, but she used her powers to captivate her prison guard. She escaped, and has been evading capture since."

I pause, remembering the things she said. "You know her."

Damian looks down.

"You were friends?" I ask

"Sort of. We were… together."

My jaw drops. "Together? Like as in boyfriend and girlfriend?"

"Look, it's not something I'm proud of." Damian shakes his head. "Let's just say that I was thinking with the wrong head."

"How did you break up?"

"My father found out and knocked some sense into me. Literally and figuratively." Damian rubs the back of his head. "It could've been a lot worse. As a royal, I'm expected to know better. I could've been banished, like your mom."

"Why weren't you?"

"My father swept it under the rug. I was never charged." Damian pauses. "Now my parents seem to think that they have the right to choose a girl for me." He shakes his head. "They might be right, though. Maybe I'm not capable of choosing the right girl. I thought I felt a connection with someone, but she turned out to be someone entirely different than who I thought she was. And Lord knows, my parents wouldn't approve of her, either."

Is he talking about Licinia? Or me? My heart flutters at the thought. "Damian, I want to explain what was happening at the club–"

"No need." He cuts me off. "I don't care."

"You saved my life. You must care a little bit!" I lower my voice. "Thank you."

He shrugs. "It was nothing."

"It was far from nothing. If you hate me so much, why did you save me?"

"My mom heard you might be in danger. She asked me to watch over you."

"Your mom?" My brow furrows.

"Our moms were best friends growing up. Does your mom ever talk about Taya Nightingale? My mom talks about your mom all the time."

I shake my head. "My mom doesn't talk about Aurelia at all. I think it hurts her to think about that time in her life."

"My mom convinced your mom to go to nursing school with her at a human university. A lot of witches choose to go to college or spend time traveling in the human realm. At that time, Aurelia was the size of a large city. Today, through more witches donating their powers, it's bigger than New Jersey. Still, it's much smaller and less diverse than the human realm. A lot of witches choose to spend months or sometimes years in the human realm, broadening their horizons. While some choose to live in the human realm permanently, many return to raise their families in Aurelia." Damian pauses. "Obviously, your mother lost the privilege of that option."

Damian takes a deep breath. "My mom blames herself for what happened to your family. She thinks that if she hadn't convinced your mom to go to college in the human realm, well, then, she wouldn't have met your dad."

"But then I wouldn't be here," I say. "So, you can tell your mom to stop beating herself up, and that I said thank you."

"I will." Damian nods. "She'll be happy to hear that."

"Even though being banished from Aurelia was devastating for her, my mom is happy with her life. She's happily married, and she loves working as a nurse at Mountainside hospital. She's saved so many lives. Sometimes, she even uses her magic to heal patients." I say with pride.

"She does WHAT?"

"She uses magic—"

"No, I heard you. I'm just shocked. Although I shouldn't be, considering that she's a human-lover." I can hear the disgust in his voice.

"What's your problem?" I can't believe that I was starting to believe that Damian could be a decent person. "I don't like that she does it, because she puts her own health at risk, but what's your issue with it?"

Damian shakes his head. "First of all, it's against the law. Statute 112-B specifically states that witches cannot use magic to either harm or heal humans, unless under exceptional circumstances which must be pre-approved by the king."

"I'm not a fan of your authoritarian society that dictates what witches can use their magic for. I believe in free will. Also, what are you, a legal encyclopedia? Are you studying to be a lawyer or something?"

Damian smirks. "Something like that. Let's just say I'm very well-versed in the law, and I can assure you that these laws are not about control, but preservation. Humans are not our friends, Zoeli. Witch hunters are everywhere. They've assembled groups that make it their life's purpose to destroy us. They're growing in numbers, and in their ability to identify us. Over fifty of our own were murdered just this past year. Burned at the stake like the Salem witch trials."

"I had no idea."

"There's a lot you don't know." Damian looks all too pleased to point out my ignorance. If he hadn't just saved my life, I might smack that smug look off his face. "That's why we can't use magic in the presence of humans. If your mother continues to miraculously heal patients, she's putting a target on her own back. And I'm not convinced that if she was being tortured, she wouldn't sell out the rest of us."

"My mother isn't a traitor!"

"If she were loyal to our people, she wouldn't have married a human." Damian's mouth tightens into a firm line. "That's why I'm so upset about your actions tonight, Zoe. What if there was a witch hunter in the club? Don't you think that half of the guys in the club following you around with their tongues hanging out of their mouths would arouse suspicion? You're putting yourself, and the rest of us, in danger. And for what? Some sick ego trip?"

"I couldn't control it!"

"You haven't had any trouble controlling your powers before."

"That's because these aren't my powers!" I blurt out.

Damian's forehead creases. "Come again?"

I stare at the ground, moonlight reflecting on my boots. "I did an evulsion."

"You did *what?*"

"I stole my sister's powers."

"This just keeps getting better."

"It's bad, I know, but not as bad as it sounds. Saria's always been more powerful than me. Aunt Gwenna called me a sitting duck. You've made it quite clear that you think I'm pathetic. Saria refused to transfer any power to me, even though she knows we're both in danger." I shake my head. "I didn't expect to take so much. I didn't even really expect it to work."

Damian's brow furrows. He studies me with eyes like black holes. I might get sucked in if I look too long. "Can I check if you're telling the truth?"

"How? Like a lie detector test?"

"Sort of. I'm going to jump into your mind for a second."

I cringe, drawing back. "My mind isn't a swimming pool."

"You'd be surprised by the similarities." The full moon illuminates Damian's masculine features: his strong jaw, straight nose, full lips. It's a shame he's so hot. We could never be together. I wouldn't want to be with an ignorant jerk like him anyway. "Do I have your consent?"

"Will it hurt?"

"Only if you resist."

I take a deep breath. I want Damian to trust me. As much as I loathe to admit it, I might need his protection again. If he hadn't shown up tonight, I would've been wolf food. "Okay."

Fire worms through my brain, growing into a fist of burning embers that clenches my skull from the inside. I stifle a scream.

"Relax." Damian's muffled voice sounds miles away. "I don't want to hurt you." His fingers interlace with mine, and suddenly, I'm calm even though my heart is beating faster than a rocket ship.

I feel him inside my head, meandering around, slow at first, the gentle tingles of a caress. Then, he moves faster, a lightning bolt racing through my veins. I can taste him: spicy and sweet, hot sauce mixed with honey.

Then, he's gone. I gasp, my arms flailing, reaching for anything to steady myself before I topple over. I wind up in his arms, nuzzling his chest: his arms strong around me, his heartbeat pulsing against my ear. "You were telling the truth," he says.

"Don't doubt me again."

"I won't." His arms tighten around me. "Are you okay?"

"I'm fine." The truth is that I feel light-headed and a bit giddy, but I'm pretty sure that has nothing to do with what just happened and everything to do with the fact that I'm in Damian's arms. His warmth permeates through my skin, setting every cell in my body on fire.

"What are you doing Saturday?"

"I don't know." I'm not sure if I even know my own name right now. What is wrong with me? This guy is a bigheaded jerk who thinks he's better than me. There's no way that I can be attracted to him! Snap out of it!

"Come with me to Aurelia. It's time for you to have a proper lesson in magical control."

"I'm not allowed."

"I'll handle that." Damian stands, lifting me up with him. "It's late. I need to get you home safely. This time, you're getting in my car. It's too long to walk."

"I was going to call an Uber." I check my phone. Now that Licinia's gone, I have full service.

"Don't even think about it." Damian grabs me by the waist and swoops me over his shoulder, Tarzan-style.

"Hey!" I'm upside down, my arms beating his back, my legs kicking in the air. "You're going to pay for this!" I try to keep my voice serious, but laughter breaks through.

"I'm not letting you out of my sight until you're home safe and sound." Damian says. "And if that means I have to kidnap you, so be it." Despite my thrashing, Damian moves fast, his hold on me secure. He flips me over, tosses me into the passenger seat of his SUV, and closes the door.

I never thought I'd like being kidnapped so much.

Chapter Fourteen

Saria

Bang! Bang! Bang! My bedroom door shakes and clatters from the impact. "Saria, wake up!" I jerk up in bed, eyeing my bedside alarm clock. 5:30am.

Heart on overdrive, I dart into the hallway. Mom's in her pajamas, pounding on the door across from mine. Bang! Bang! Bang! "Zoeli, wake up, now!"

"What the hell's going on?"

"Family meeting! Everyone up and in the magic room, now!"

Oh, no. When Zoeli didn't come home until after I was in bed last night, I'd hoped she would forget. I don't know why she's so intent on sharing my problems with Zoeli. It's not like she's going to care. She'll probably laugh at me.

"Come on, Mom," I say. "I need to sleep. School's in two hours."

"That's why we need to get started. We don't have much time."

I didn't sleep much last night. After Logan brought me home, some of my friends reached out. Keisha texted me to check in. Penny called multiple times to see if I needed anything, her voice fraught with worry. Even without my powers, they're true friends.

Giselle called, and while she was concerned, she was also excited. Giselle pitched a fabulous game. It turns out the Panthers don't need me to win after all.

After we hung up, I lay awake for hours, tossing and turning, webs of emotions tangling inside me. The huge mass buzzed with rage, fear, remorse, but also relief. Overwhelmed by the chaos, my emotions came untethered, rising into my throat, blocking my airway. Gasping for air, I dissolved into a full-blown panic attack, blankets twisted around me, sweat soaking through my pajamas.

Then, I remembered what Logan said, "This could be an opportunity for you to grow. Embrace it." I breathed evenly until my heart rate slowed down, and then I got to work: unraveling the threads, one by one, uncovering the origin of each, trying to figure myself out. Part of me feels like a weight has been lifted. My team won without me. My failure didn't impact them.

Another part of me is devastated. But why? Is it because I miss being the star, the applause, the adulation? Or is it because I love softball? A long time ago, I would've thought the latter. Now, I'm not so sure. I close my eyes and visualize myself on the field, my cleats digging into the clay, diving to make a catch, the perfect crack of a bat hitting the ball, the rush of adrenaline as I slide into home plate. I do love the game. I just don't love the player I've become: greedy, selfish, a show-off, fake.

Maybe I'll take the rest of this season off. Someone else can take my spot on the team, someone who deserves it. I'll practice every chance I get. I'll go to the batting cages every day. Next season, I'll try out for the team, using nothing but my true abilities.

It's time for me to find myself, test myself and discover what I'm truly made of. If any of my friendships fall apart, I'll let them go, knowing they were never real in the first place. Last night, Logan said, "This could be the best thing that ever happened to you." He might be right.

I lift my chin and follow Mom down the stairs and into the magic room. It's time to face the music. Dad sits up straight on the couch, the broken window behind him. I guess Aunt Gwenna hasn't fixed the damage she caused yet. Mom sits beside him, her hands in her lap.

I settle into the large armchair, leaning back and taking in all the magical tools that surround me. Rows of containers are filled with ingredients used for magical potions. Beside them, an intricate statue of a crow perches on a branch, its eyes green and otherworldly, like my mother's. It's funny how I'd always assumed it was just a cute decoration, a play on our last name.

Footsteps creak in the hallway, and then Zoeli appears. There's something different about her. Head down, Zoeli's hair falls in waves around her shoulders. It's lush and shiny, like she just had it done. She lingers in the doorframe, shifting from foot to foot, wringing her hands.

"Zoe, do you have something to tell your sister?"

"I'm sorry." Zoe keeps her gaze on the floor.

"For what?" My brow furrows.

Zoeli looks up. Her skin is glowing: dewy and flushed. Her eyes glimmer: flecks of green glow inside aquamarine blue irises. It hits me all at once like a freight train pummeling off the rails and catapulting into a gas station. Something explodes inside of me, blasting apart and rising to the surface. "You did this."

My fury burns hot and fast, quickly dissolving in the ocean of opposing emotions: sadness, guilt and shame. Tears run down my cheeks. Zoeli and I used to stay up all night making shadow puppets and braiding each other's hair. We always played a game where we'd make up silly stories and tell them to each other with a straight face. Whoever laughed first was the loser. By the end of the game, we'd both be rolling on the floor, the happiest losers that I ever knew. What happened to us?

"What Zoeli did was wrong," Mom says. "Your powers will be returned to you, Saria. Gwenna will assist to make sure that the transfer is done safely and effectively."

I stand frozen, my mouth open, but no words form. It's a tempting offer. If my powers are restored, everything will go back to normal. But I don't want to go back. I want to move forward. I want to grow. I shake my head. "No."

Zoeli's jaw drops. "What?"

Mom nods. "I thought this would happen. Gwenna and I discussed it last night, and we realized that the evulsion would've never been successful unless Saria wanted it to be. Tell me what's going on, Saria."

Zoeli throws her hands in the air. "I can't get credit for anything around here!"

Dad folds his arms across his chest. "You broke the law, stole from your sister and almost killed yourself in the process. That's not something to be proud of," Dad says. Zoe's gaze falls to the floor. Mom watches me, waiting.

"I, I…" I pause, trying to find the words. "I think I became too dependent on my powers. I was using them a lot more than I should."

"We noticed at the game last night," Dad says.

I wince, humiliation washing over me. I've been exposed as a fraud. My parents must be so disappointed in me. "I, I, I don't always have control over it."

Dad raises his eyebrows. "You're telling me that fastballs fly out of your hands at lightning speed of their own accord?"

"Um, no, not exactly." I take a deep breath. It's time to come clean. "I willfully used my powers to enhance my performance in softball. I've also used them to make people do what I want and make myself look prettier."

"Which you know is unacceptable," Dad starts, but Mom holds up her hand.

"Let her finish."

"But, sometimes, I don't do it on purpose," I say. "Sometimes people just seem to fall under my thrall, and I don't have any control over it."

"After you turned thirteen and your powers fully came in, we went over strategies to suppress your powers," Mom says.

"They didn't work." I study the scratches on the old wood floor.

"Why didn't you tell me?"

I shrug. "Because I liked it." My cheeks redden. I'm embarrassed that I was so shallow. "I enjoyed the attention." I pause, digging deeper, reflecting on my own actions. "Everyone always praised me for being good at everything. It got to that point that admitting I couldn't do something felt like a failure. I felt like I had to be perfect, or that I was letting everyone down."

"Saria," Mom says. "No one expects you to be perfect. We love you. We want you to come to us when you need help."

"Okay." I nod, tears streaming down my cheeks.

"So tonight we'll do the transfer–"

"No." I shake my head. "I need this." My voice comes out garbled, desperate. "I need to see who my real friends are. I want to see if Mallory and Penny and Chad…" My voice trails off. "I just need this."

"I understand," Mom says. "But you need to be safe. Talon's militia is–"

"Didn't Gwenna say that she's been watching over Saria? Along with her daughter Caliah?" Dad says.

"Yes, but they can't be there all the time."

"Gwenna said that there's another royal who spends a lot of time on this side. Colson Nightingale, I think it was. He could help, too," Dad says.

"John, the powers belong to Saria! They need to be returned to their rightful owner. It's the law."

"I'm not disagreeing," Dad says. "I'm just suggesting that maybe we could give her a little bit more time to figure things out. A few weeks, perhaps?"

"Yes, please," I croak out, so grateful for my dad.

"I'll think about it," Mom says. "But you'd better not complain when flocks of birds trail you everywhere you go." She checks her watch. "It's time for me to get ready for work. If you notice anything suspicious, text me right away. We all have to stay on guard."

A short while later, Giselle's Range Rover rolls up the driveway. Mallory sits up front. I slide into the back seat next to Penny. "How are you feeling?" Penny asks, her hazel eyes wide with concern.

"Okay," I say. "Better than yesterday."

Mallory spins around and lowers her sunglasses to the bridge of her nose. She studies me, her eyes twinkling. A smirk touches her lips. "You still look like garbage."

My cheeks heat up, rage boiling in my gut. If Zoeli hadn't admitted to the evulsion, I'd be sure that Mallory had something to do with it. My gut tells me that something's off with that girl. Aunt Gwenna even said that a witch has been toying with me, making me feel unbalanced. Is it possible that the witch has been messing with Zoeli too? Maybe even planting ideas in her head?

"Mallory!" Penny scolds. "That's mean!" She puts her hand on mine. "You look great, Sar."

I smile at Penny, my heart slowing down. "Thanks, Pen." It feels good to have a true friend.

Mallory rolls her eyes. "I was kidding around. Some people can't take a joke, I guess."

"Giselle, I want to hear all about the game," I say, even though I already got the play-by-play on the phone last night. Giselle deserves to relish in this moment.

"Are you sure?" Giselle says. "I don't want to make you feel worse."

"I'm sure," I say. "I'm so happy for you."

Along the winding, bumpy ride to school, Giselle shares every last nail-biting detail of the game, and how the Panthers won by the skin of their teeth. It was the most exciting game of the season. One that the team will talk about for years to come. They came together, fought and came out victorious. Without me.

***

"Ugh, I suck!" I slam my bat on the ground in frustration. "Another whiff." I shake my head.

In the batting cage beside mine, Logan swings. He makes contact, the ball whizzing into the wall with a thud.

"Nice hit," I mumble. "I'm pathetic."

"Will you stop putting yourself down?" Logan says, swinging again. I can't help but notice his biceps flexing through the swing. For a skinny guy, he's got some nice definition. "It's our first practice. Did you think that you'd be knocking them all out of the park?"

"Yes," I admit, my head down. "I'm not used to failing."

"In time, you'll get good at it."

"Failing or hitting?"

"Both." Logan grins. "As a mere mortal, I confess that I've failed more times than I can count."

"Really?" I swing and miss. "What's your biggest failure?

Logan shrugs. "I thought I was in love once, but she didn't feel the same way." He swings. The ball dings against the edge of his bat, sailing behind him.

"She's a fool. One day she'll kick herself for missing out on the chance to be with you." I swing too late, my bat whizzing alone in space. "I suck!" I throw my bat on the ground. "This is hopeless!"

"Are you done berating yourself?" Logan asks.

I shake my head. "Probably not."

Logan stands his bat up on the side of the cage. "There's something in my trunk that I want to show you."

"It better not be a dead body. I have enough to deal with at the moment." I follow Logan into the parking lot. He clicks a button on his keychain and his trunk pops open. Inside, two leafy green plants sit side-by-side inside matching white ceramic pots. Logan picks up one of the plants and hands it to me.

"What's this for?"

"Our science project." Logan holds up a piece of paper. "Here's instructions on how to care for the plant. I want you to follow them exactly, except I want you to do one other thing."

"What's that?"

"I want you to yell at your plant every day."

"Excuse me?"

"Every insult, every negative belief, every belittling or self-deprecating thought you have throughout the day. Hold it in and save it up. Then, at night, unleash it all in a brutal tongue-lashing at your plant."

"That's weird." I rub my chin. "And unhinged. If anyone sees me, I'll end up institutionalized."

"Then keep your curtains closed." Logan presses the instructions into my palm. "There's a method to my madness. Trust the process."

I shrug. "I guess it won't be the craziest thing I've ever done."

"That's the spirit." Logan slaps me on the back.

"And next time I ask you to do something completely ridiculous, you'd better be game."

"Deal." We shake on it.

"Payback's a bitch. I'll be plotting my revenge."

"If your plotting skills are anything like your batting skills, I've got nothing to worry about."

"Hey!" I swing my fist, aiming to play-punch him. Logan ducks, and grabs me around my waist. He wrestles me against his car, our bodies pressed together. My heart pounds. His breath tickles my ear, sending shivers down my spine.

"Saria?" Mallory stands at the edge of our parking spot, leaning on her bat like a cane. "What are you doing?"

Logan and I spring apart, like guilty lovers. "We were just, um, practicing, um, hitting."

Mallory smirks. "Looks like someone's about to score a homerun. I wonder how Chad would feel about that."

"Mal, it's not what it looks like." I say. "We're just friends." But she's already walking away, a bounce in her step, her bat swung over her shoulder. "She's always lurking around," I tell Logan. "I swear she's following me. She wants to ruin my life. She even insinuated that I'm cheating on my boyfriend!" I throw my hands up. "That's absurd!"

Logan opens his car door. "Let's go. I'll take you home." He's silent on the ride, his mouth pressed in a tight line.

When he parks at my front door, I put my hand on his arm. "Thanks for practicing with me," I say. "Same time again tomorrow?"

"Yeah, sure," he says. "Sounds good." Logan's smile doesn't reach his eyes.

Chapter Fifteen

Zoeli

A tendril of sun stretches through the space between my curtains, glistening in the darkness. I stretch out in bed, a smile spreading across my face. It's Saturday morning. Finally. It feels like I've been waiting forever.

I couldn't sleep last night: my whole body buzzed with excitement every time I closed my eyes. Today I'm going to Aurelia. It's an opportunity I never imagined I'd see in this lifetime.

Down the hallway, Mom steps in the shower, her melodic humming mingling with the steady pulse of water hitting the tile wall. Since I stole Saria's powers, my hearing is supernatural. If I focus, I can hear mice scurrying across the attic, Saria rustling beneath her covers, and a creek babbling deep inside the woods. In the middle of the night, I thought I heard a bird singing.

In less than an hour, Mom'll leave for work. It's perfect. I don't even have to make up a story. By the time Damian gets here, Mom will be long gone.

I thought about telling Mom about the expedition that Damian has planned for me, but decided against it. Mom might say it's too dangerous, and not let me go. The witches from Aurelia hate nimwit half-breeds like me. This could even be a trap. It's a risk I'm willing to take.

After Mom leaves, I get dressed and go outside. I lay in the yard, grass tickling my face every time the wind blows. Beneath me, roots spread through the dirt, curling around rocks, weaving through burrows occupied by a mother rabbit nursing her kits. Deep in the core of the earth, I hear Mother Nature's heartbeat. It syncs with my own, pulsating in my ears, harmonizing with the suckles of the kits, melding with the wind chimes that sway in the breeze. Everything is interconnected.

An engine roars and then comes to a stop. A car door opens and shuts, and then Damian lays beside me. I roll on my side and study him: his endless lashes, enormous black eyes, square jawline. "This world is beautiful," I say.

"Wait until you see Aurelia." He stands up in one swift motion. His hand reaches out towards me. I take his hand, he lifts me up, pulling me closer than necessary as my feet touch the ground. He towers above me, his massive form casting a dark shadow over me.

"Let's go," I say, sounding more confident than I feel.

We climb into his SUV. Damian steps on the gas, and we're off. One back road leads to another, and twenty minutes later, there's no sign of civilization. We zoom around winding paths, pebbles crunching under the tires.

Once we're completely off road, the sides of Damian's SUV scraping against bushes, tree branches snapping off against the windshield, sweat beads along my hairline. This scene is straight out of a horror movie. I'm the dumb girl who got in the car with the handsome guy, only to be driven into the depths of the woods, murdered and dismembered. If he attacks me, I'll go down fighting. Hands wringing in my lap, I mentally prepare myself for the next step. I'm ready for war.

"What's wrong?" Damian looks over at me, his brow furrowed.

"Where are we?"

"You didn't think the portal to Aurelia was right out in the open for anyone to find, did you?" I hate when he speaks to me in that condescending tone, like I'm a moron. Even though there's moments when he's nice to me, the truth is that I'm just a half-breed nimwit in his eyes. I clench my fists, my knuckles turning white. Part of me hopes that this is a trap. I'd love to bash in his perfectly sculpted jaw, and then slap that haughty grin right off his plump kissable lips. What's wrong with me? The dichotomy of my feelings for Damian might drive me insane.

Despite being repelled by his arrogance, part of me feels inexplicably drawn to him. Some nights, I can't stop thinking about him. It's almost like he set a spell on me. At the end of the day, I'm not going to fall for him. I know better. I deserve better.

Damian turns onto a patch of overgrown grass, and then turns off the ignition. "Get out."

There's no trails out here. We step over rocks, around trees, and through bushes, branches snagging my clothes and scratching my skin. Damian helps me over a huge boulder, and then down a ravine.

I turn back, a labyrinth of dense forest in my wake. I'll never find my way back. If I run now, I'll sentence myself to a long and agonizing death. We trudge through mud, dirt caking on the bottoms of my jeans, for what feels like forever.

Finally, Damian stops. He crouches next to a tree that's larger than the rest, its branches sprawling out like a canopy above us. An "A" is carved on its massive trunk. Damian brushes a pile of leaves aside. Using his pointer, he draws on the dirt, his finger moving in a rapid succession. "What are you doing?" I ask.

"It's a password of sorts." Beneath his finger, a golden door materializes. It could be a portal to a magical kingdom… or a grave. "Here it is," Damian says. "Do you want to do the honors?" He gestures to the golden handle.

I shake my head. "I don't know what that is. I'm not waking up a vampire."

Damian swings the door open. Thousands of multi-color sparkles swirl in the entrance, like rainbows that have come to life. "Does it look like vampires live here?"

I shrug. "Vampire unicorns, maybe." I step closer, looking down into the whirlpool of colors, wondering what's underneath.

Damian takes my hand. Sparks shoot through my fingertips. "Together," he says. "On the count of three. One, two, three."

I jump. Glowing gems swirl around me, like a blanket of shooting stars. Comets race by, blue moons eclipse, and purple planets twirl on their orbits. We're leaving this dimension, traveling through space at the speed of light. "Watch out!" Damian's voice echoes in the dark. I'm enamored by meteors sailing by. Enormous chunks of ruby and amethyst glimmer, lighting up the blackness of the vortex. "Look down!" I hear the urgency in Damian's tone, but I can't look away.

Crash! I land on my back, a cloud of brown dust rising from the impact. Damian leans over me, waving the dust away. "You okay?" he asks, laughing as he holds out his hand.

I swat his hand away, and stand up on my own. He's still laughing. "That wasn't funny," I say.

"Not for you." Damian retorts. "But from my vantage point, it was hysterical."

"Jerk," I mutter under my breath, brushing the dirt off my jeans.

"Hey, I tried to warn you." The space around us is barren. Dirt paths and gray skies are all I see.

"This is it?" I ask.

"We're not there yet," Damian says. "We have to pass the border." We walk along the dirt path, the air eerily still and quiet. As we make our way over a hill, a white sign with red letters comes into view.

WITCHES ONLY

A chill runs down my spine. I'm not welcome here. As if their point wasn't already abundantly clear, a second sign is erected only a few feet away.

NO HUMANS
NO HALF-BREEDS
TURN BACK NOW
OR FACE THE CONSEQUENCES

A few yards ahead, old-fashioned cannons are stationed on top of an enormous wall. At least a dozen blue-clad soldiers swarm in front of the entrance, machine guns strapped across their chests.

My heart rises into my throat, restricting my airway. I gasp for air; my head feels fuzzy. "We have to go back," I say.

"Don't worry about them," Damian says.

"They'll kill me!"

"No, they won't," Damian says. "You're with me." Maybe this was his plan all along. Maybe he never intended to kill me himself, but allow them to do it for him.

"And just who do you think you– "

"I am honored, Prince Nightingale." The soldier bows before Damian. My jaw falls open. The soldier turns to me. "And you are?" His name is embroidered into a yellow strip above his chest pocket, MILLER.

"Um, um," I stammer.

"Zoeli McKinney-Crowe," Damian answers for me. "The King and Queen have given special permission for her to enter Aurelia today."

"McKinney-Crowe, huh?" Officer Miller spits out my name as if it's a curse. I cringe and step backwards. "I'll be right back." Officer Miller trots back over to the group of soldiers.

"Why didn't you tell me that you're a prince?" I ask.

Damian shrugs. "I liked that you didn't know. Everyone around here treats me like the sun shines out of my ass. It was nice to be… normal."

"So, you like it when I argue with you and call you a jerk?"

"When you put it that way…"

Officer Miller and another soldier march back towards us. Officer Miller grabs my upper arm, his fingers digging into my flesh. "Ow!" I shout, trying to pull away. He clutches my arm harder.

"Anderson, get the other side," Miller orders.

Officer Anderson snags my other arm, twisting until it hurts. His gaze moves up and down my body, stopping at my breasts. He licks his lips. "She's not bad for a nimwit. I reckon that I'll have a little fun with her before we throw her in the dungeon."

I can't break free, so I spit in his face. A wad of saliva lands on his nose. "You disgusting little half-breed!" He raises his arm to punch me, but Damian catches his fist before it strikes.

"What the hell do you think you're doing?"

"Prince Nightingale, sir," Officer Anderson replies. "Our orders are to send half-breeds directly to the dungeon."

"I've already explained to you that this is a special case." Damian speaks through clenched teeth. "Let go of her."

"We're doing our job," Anderson says.

"Once this is straightened out, neither of you will have jobs," Damian threatens. "Now get your filthy hands off her before I make you."

"We're just following protocol," Miller says. "If your parents want to release her from the dungeon, that's their call."

"I'm only going to say it one more time," Damian says. "Let her go."

Another soldier darts over, waving his hands in the air. "Stop! I just spoke to Queen Taya herself. Ms. McKinney-Crowe is permitted to enter Aurelia with Damian as her chaperone."

"Why weren't we informed sooner?" Miller asks.

"King Keifer meant to put the order in this morning, but it must've slipped his mind. The queen just put the order through. The girl should not be harmed."

Miller lets go of my arm. I shake it out, my fingers stinging as blood flow returns. Anderson isn't as gentle when he releases me. As he lets go, he shoves me. I stumble, tripping over my own feet before Damian catches me. "You're not only going to be fired, Anderson. I'm going to see to it that you spend the next decade behind bars."

Miller squares on Damian. "I didn't do anything wrong. The orders hadn't gone through."

"Use of excessive force. Sexual harassment. Lewd and obscene threats."

"No one will care about the way I treated a half-breed!"

"I'll file the charges myself if I have to," Damian says. "Come on, Zoe. Let's go."

"Taya Nightingale is nothing but a stupid liberal," Anderson says. "King Keifer would've never allowed this if it wasn't for his half-breed-loving wife."

"It's a slippery slope," Miller agrees. "We let one in, and before we know it, they'll be coming in by the boatload, threatening our way of life."

"The Nightingales should've never been appointed as king and queen. When the Crowes were dethroned, the Lyons should've taken over."

"I swear that vote was rigged."

Hand-in-hand, Damian and I move forward. The rest of the soldiers step aside, allowing us to pass. We step through the gap and into Aurelia, the land of power and bigots.

Chapter Sixteen

Zoeli

Initially, I'm disappointed. Aurelia doesn't look very different from earth. We walk along the sidewalk until we reach the corner where a limousine waits.

I slide into the limo behind Damian. Inside, he opens a stocked mini-fridge. "Do you want a soda?"

"I'd love one." The cold liquid feels like heaven sliding down my parched throat.

"Prince Nightingale, sir. Where to?" Up front, a chauffeur stares back at us from underneath a flat cap.

"Enchantments Academy, Oliver."

Oliver hits the gas, and the limo takes off. Through the window, Aurelia flies by. Apartment buildings, stores and roads that look like home. Then, it changes. Gradually, at first, and then rapidly.

The colors of the sky shift: from a gravelly gray, to a clear ocean blue, to lavender mixed with blue, and finally into a sky streaked with so many colors that it looks like the northern lights streaked with rainbows.

Underneath the gravel sky, witches walk or jog, their feet firmly rooted to the ground. Closer to the multi-colored sky, gravity is less restrictive. A street performer dances in the air. A witch floats over our limo to cross the street.

I point, words not coming to me. "What? How?" I sound like a bumbling idiot.

"As we get closer to Aurelia's power source, the world becomes more magical," Damian explains. "On the outskirts, the magic isn't as strong."

The limousine turns onto a road composed of glowing gems. We veer around a curve, and a building unlike anything I've seen before comes into view. The building is at least twenty stories high, and slanted at a forty-five-degree angle. It's made from bricks that look like diamonds.

"It's really something, isn't it?"

"And I thought the Leaning Tower of Pisa was cool." I stare in awe. "This is…wow."

The limousine lurches to a stop. Within moments, Oliver opens the back door. "We've reached your destination, Prince Nightingale."

"What?" I shake my head. "This is your school?" I take Oliver's hand and he helps me out. Enchantments Academy glistens in the sun. I squint and shield my eyes with my hands. "Why was it built this way?"

"What do you mean?" Damian asks. "It's awesome."

"I agree that it's aesthetically pleasing," I say. "But I was wondering if there's any utility to the design.'

Damian grins. "Nah, we just like to show off." It's Saturday, so the school grounds are empty. "I asked Ms. Apotheker to meet me here. She's one of the lead instructors. She's also one of my mom's best friends, and good at keeping a secret. Otherwise, we'd be all over the tabloids tomorrow."

As we get closer to the building, I realize that the building isn't actually made of diamonds, but intricately-cut crystals that sparkle in the sun. Up close, it's even more breathtaking.

Ms. Apotheker waits by the entrance, her flowy skirt swaying in the breeze. "Welcome, Zoeli, it's a pleasure to meet you." Two tiny braids pull her blonde hair away from her face, secured with a beaded barrette. She extends her hand. "Your mother was my classmate, many moons ago."

"Thank you for meeting us here," I say, taking her hand. After what happened at the border, I didn't expect respect or kindness from an Aurelian. I relax a little.

"I'm happy to help." We step inside a foyer so opulent that I'm sure we're in the wrong place. There's no way this can be a school. Under my sneakers, white marble floors glisten. Above us, a mural of nightingales floating in trees covers the dome-shaped ceiling. "This way," Ms. Apotheker says.

Ding! Gold doors drift apart, and we step inside the elevator. Ms. Apotheker presses the button for the seventeenth floor. As they chat about people who I know nothing about, I can't help but feel like I don't belong here. Part of me hoped that coming to Aurelia would feel like coming home, but I feel just as alien here as I do on earth. I guess that's the tough part about being a half-breed. No matter where I go, half of me will belong somewhere else.

"Damian tells me that you're having trouble controlling your powers," Ms. Apotheker says. The elevator dings, and the doors open. "I'm going to help you with that today." We walk down a long corridor. The walls are decorated with peculiar art: portraits of kings and queens, sculptures of beasts, paintings of scenes that must have significance, but I don't recognize.

At the end of the hallway, Ms. Apotheker flicks her finger, and a door opens. As Damian and Ms. Apotheker slip inside the room, I trail behind, studying a painting just outside the classroom door. A blue-clad soldier drives a stake into the heart of a vampiress, blood-stained fangs protruding from her mouth. It's a depiction of the great witch-vampire war that Damian told me about. Goosebumps sprout on my skin.

"Zoe." Damian holds the door open. "Come in."

I lift my chin and go in. Damian slides behind a desk, and motions for me to take the one next to him. He leans back in his chair, and gives me a lazy grin. His sheer size dwarfs the chair and everything around him. I can only imagine how much attention he gets at school. He's handsome, muscular AND a prince. The girls must go crazy for him. Not that I care. Because I don't care. Not at all.

Ms. Apotheker sits in a chair opposite me. "Tell me what's going on, Zoeli."

I open my mouth, and then shut it, unsure of how much to say. I glance over at Damian. "I told her everything," Damian says.

"Yes, but I want to hear it from you," Ms. Apotheker says. "What seems to be the problem, Zoeli?"

"Well, before…" I pause. Ms. Apotheker nods for me to continue. "Before I did the evulsion and stole my sister's powers, I had a really hard time accessing my powers. I had pretty much given up." I stare at my hands, ashamed of my weakness. "Since the evulsion, the magic feels like it's overflowing. I can't suppress it. I'm bewitching people without any effort at all."

Ms. Apotheker looks thoughtful. "I would like to put you inside the Power Scanner, if you don't mind. It will give us a better idea of what's going on."

"Power scanner?" I follow Ms. Apotheker's gaze to a human-sized translucent cylinder standing in the corner.

"Think of it like a CT scan, but for magic," Damian says. "There's no side effects. You won't feel anything."

"Okay, I guess." Ms. Apotheker leads me to the scanner. She moves soundlessly, her ballet flats almost drifting over the tiles. When she presses a button, the cylinder splits open. "Go in." Palms clammy, I step forward. The chamber whirs, and the halves click back together. I'm locked inside. "Hands by your sides. Stay very still."

A motor roars. On the wall, a screen lights up. I recognize the shape of my body. First, it's an empty outline, and then it fills with color. Orange and yellow takes up most of the space, lustrous color spreading from my fingertips, down my legs and into my toes. In my center, a small mass of deep blue glimmers, like ocean waves glistening in the sun.

Ms. Apotheker raises her brows. "Very interesting." She strokes her chin. "It all makes sense now." She points to the screen. "The orange and yellow magic belongs to Saria. The blue is Zoeli's magic."

I groan. "That's it? Saria has like, a million times more power than me."

"It's not that simple." Ms. Apotheker presses a button. The screen turns black and the chamber opens. "Come on out and I'll explain it to you." I step out and perch on the edge of a desk. I'm ready for the verdict.

"All magic isn't created equal. Orange magic is the easiest to access. When a witch wants to use magic, orange and yellow will flow easily, like an artery bursting open. Blue magic is different. It's much harder to access, but once you find it, its strength is unsurmountable. It is the most powerful of any magic."

My jaw falls open. "What?"

"Your power, the blue magic, could cause far more good…. or damage, than all of Saria's powers combined."

"Not if I can't even use it," I grumble.

"With practice, you may be able to access it, but blue magic seems to have a will of its own. It doesn't like to be used for frivolous purposes. It seems to reserve itself for instances of life-and-death or battles of good versus evil. Once it releases itself, it's a force to be reckoned with.

"Think of it like fire. The flames closest to the surface are orange, but the root, the hottest part, is blue."

A force to be reckoned with. The words echo in my brain. *I'm* stronger than Saria. It's unbelievable. I grimace as I realize that the evulsion was unnecessary. If Ms. Apotheker's right, I can defend myself better than Saria can. I might not be able to seduce strangers or win a beauty pageant, but if it comes down to a battle, I'll kick some ass.

"If you'd attended Enchantments Academy, we would've discovered this years ago. We would've taught Saria how to suppress her powers. With her excess of yellow and orange magic, there's no doubt that she's struggled. For you, Zoeli, we could've worked on strategies to help you reach your blue magic."

"But half-breeds aren't invited to attend the academy," Damian says.

"And this scan proves how ridiculous that rule is!" Ms. Apotheker says. "There are full-blooded witches with less inherited magic than you."

"Really?" My eyes widen.

"Sometimes full-blooded witches are born with little to no powers. We call them duds." Damian shrugs. "They mostly fail out of the academy. If they choose to stay in Aurelia, they live on the outskirts in low-income housing and work menial jobs."

"That's awful," I say. "Just because of how they're born, they don't have a chance."

"It isn't much different on Earth, from what I understand," Damian says.

"Magical genetics is a new field of study. We still have a lot to learn about how it works." Ms. Apotheker's forehead wrinkles. "The distribution of magic between you and Saria is very unusual. I wonder if something went awry in the womb, being that you're twins. Maybe the colors were meant to meld together, but when the egg split into two, the colors split apart too."

I turn to face Damian. "What color magic do you have?"

"Purple," Damian's lips curve into his trademark cocky grin. "A combo of blue and red. As you know, blue is the most powerful. Mixing in red makes the blue more accessible, therefore making purple the most desirable form of magic."

Ms. Apotheker cuts in. "While many might agree with you, Damian, keep in mind that pure blue will almost always beat purple during battle." As Damian's smile falls, Ms. Apotheker winks at me. It's hard to resist jumping out of my seat and kissing her cheek.

Ms. Apotheker hunts through her desk drawer, items clanging together before she pulls out a device that looks like a smart watch. "This caliper will help guide you as you learn to suppress the overflowing magic." She snaps it on my wrist. "Your goal should be to keep the number under 200 at all times." We watch as the number on the screen soars upwards, 500, 800, 1000, and finally stopping at 1533. Ms. Apotheker rubs her eyes and looks again, as if she can't quite believe it. "Let's lower the goal number for now. We'll start by trying to keep it below 1000."

"How?"

"Through visualization, but it cannot be forced. It must come to you." Ms. Apotheker strides towards the door, her silky skirt billowing around her. "Come. We'll go to the visualization lab."

Ms. Apotheker moves ahead, Damian and I following behind. "I'm impressed." Damian's lips curve into a smile. "Blue power is nothing to mess around with."

"I told you not to underestimate me. Next time we're in trouble, maybe I'll save you."

"Not a chance, sweetheart."

"Worried I'll emasculate you? What will everyone say when they find out that the half-breed nimwit is just as powerful as the Prince of Aurelia?"

"Don't call yourself that." Damian narrows his eyes.

"Why?" I ask. "You do."

"I was wrong," Damian says. "And I'm sorry."

"Did hell just freeze over?"

"When I'm king, I'm going to make some changes around here."

"Will half-breeds be allowed in Aurelia?" I ask.

"Not all of them," Damian says. "But your family will be."

"If all half-breeds aren't welcome, I don't want special treatment."

"What do you mean?" Damian asks. His brow furrows in confusion.

"After today, I won't be coming back to Aurelia. I don't want anything to do with a country that discriminates against my kind," I say. "Deciding that I'm an exception doesn't make you any less prejudiced."

"This way," Ms. Apotheker says. Inside the visualization lab, rows of oversized plush chairs fill the room. Cherry wood cabinets line the front wall. Ms. Apotheker opens a cabinet, shuffling through its contents. She chooses a few glass jars, placing them on the white quartz countertop. "Go," Ms. Apotheker waves us away as she examines a vial of green liquid. "Choose whatever station you like."

I sink into the cushions of a blue recliner, resisting the urge to sigh. The soft material molds to my form, supporting every muscle and relieving every ache that I never knew I had. If I melt and become one with this chair, I won't mind.

Beside me, a black cauldron hangs from a metal tripod. Ms. Apotheker kneels beside it, arranging a circular bed of stones underneath. With one flick of her pointer finger, Ms. Apotheker lights a fire beneath the cauldron. She prepares a potion: pouring vials of liquid into the cauldron and stirring. She sprinkles in herbs and flower petals.

"What are you making?" I ask, hoping it's not a stupid question.

"These fumes help bring forth visions," Ms. Apotheker says. "Lay back and shut your eyes. Put your hand on your belly and breathe in until your belly fills up like a balloon, and then release."

Eyes closed, I breathe deeply. My nose tickles as the aroma enters: sweet and woodsy, mud and jasmine, damp bark and peppermint. It intensifies, burning in my throat.

"Can you feel your magic?" Ms. Apotheker asks.

I nod. It rushes beneath my skin, like waves crashing on the sand.

"Focus on that and only that. Tune everything else out. Breathe in, and breathe out. Are you seeing anything?"

I shake my head.

"Some witches see a dial, almost like a thermostat or a dimmer switch that you can turn up or down. Others have described a fire that can burn higher or lower."

"I don't see anything."

"The elixir is more potent when taken orally." I open my eyes as Ms. Apotheker dips a ladle into the cauldron. She fills up a teacup and hands it to me. I slip one finger through the tiny handle. "Drink," she says. Steam swirls up from the cauldron, filling the room with white mist. When I lift my head to drink, the room spins around me. My head weighs a million tons. I bring the cup to my lips. As the potion pours down my throat, it occurs to me that it could be poison. I could be falling right into their trap.

It stings going down, searing in my gut. I gag, and the world turns black.

Chapter Seventeen

Zoeli

I'm plummeting through open space, sailing far away. Where am I? I reach out for an anchor, but my fingers slip through nothingness. "Zoeli, can you hear me?" A voice comes from somewhere very far away. "Zoeli!" Damian's voice is louder now, but something isn't right. "Come back to us, Zoe." His words are garbled.

Colors and shapes meld into faces: smiles with too many teeth, long fangs and glowing red eyes circle around me. My heart races like a runaway train. "Zoeli!" Millions of mouths open wide. Jagged teeth, sharp as knives, gleam. "Zoeli, come back."

Come back from where? I can't remember where I was last or how I got here. This is a dream, I tell myself. This can't be real. All I have to do is open my eyes.

But I can't. It feels like my eyes are coated with cement. Sealed shut forever. I try to scream but plaster sticks in my throat. Wake up, wake up, wake up…

My eyes fly open. Back in the visualization lab, Damian leans over me, wearing an expression I've never seen before. A worry line draws a long crease between his eyebrows. His huge eyes are unblinking, devoid of their usual cocky twinkle. In fact, his entire macho persona is gone, his swagger replaced by raw, unbridled fear. "Are you okay?" His fingers lace through mine and squeeze.

"I think so. What happened?"

"She gave you too much potion." Damian glares at Ms. Apotheker accusingly. "Zoe could've died because of your negligence."

Ms. Apotheker waves her hand. "Oh, nonsense. She had a mild reaction. If her life was in danger, I would've injected her with the antidote."

"How long was I out?" I ask.

"A few minutes," Ms. Apotheker answers. "You're fine. He's overdramatic." Ms. Apotheker shifts her gaze to Damian's hand, still interlocked with mine. "If I didn't know better, I'd think…" She shakes her head. "Let's continue with the exercise."

"I think Zoe's had enough for today," Damian says. "She needs a break."

"I think you're the one who needs a break," I say, surveying Damian's ashen skin. Maybe he does care about me. It's more likely that he's just worried about the consequences if I get hurt on his watch. His mom asked him to protect me. His fragile male ego might shatter if he failed at his assigned duty. "I want to continue."

I settle back into the plush cushions, and put my hand on my belly. "Fill your belly up with air, and then let it out," Ms. Apotheker says. "Slow, controlled, measured breaths. Focus on your magic, and only your magic. Drown everything else out."

I'm on a hill, pushing a gigantic boulder. Inside the semi-translucent yellow-orange rock, there's a small blue nucleus. My fingers burn on the blazing hot surface; my forehead scrunches up as I bear the pain.

If I let go, it will roll over me, almost certain to flatten me like a pancake. The only way to go is up. I peer around it, searching for the top of the hill, and realize that it's more like a mountain. There's no end in sight.

I use all of the force I can muster: using hands, arms and elbows, then my hips. I thrust my entire body weight into it. It won't budge. I take a deep breath, stepping back and then launching myself forward. I take one baby step forward. I try again, this time taking two steps. I catapult myself even harder, and make it another few feet forward.

I look beyond the boulder, and I grimace. The path seems endless. I'll never make it. My hands are scorching. If this was the real world, they would have blackened and disintegrated by now. I can't do it. I give up. I fail.

I open my eyes. "It's useless," I say. "I'm not strong enough."

"Nonsense, dear." Ms. Apotheker holds up my wrist with one hand, and points to the magical caliper with the other. "It's down to 1000." I shift my gaze to my wrist. "Try to hold on," Ms. Apotheker says. "Don't break your concentration."

But I've already quit. I watch the numbers rise: 1022, 1103, 1356, and back up to 1500. "It's okay." Ms. Apotheker puts her hand on my shoulder. "That was an excellent first try, especially considering the unusual amount of magic that you're up against. Great job." I can't decide if she's patronizing me.

A thin layer of sweat glazes my forehead. "It's so much effort," I say. "How am I supposed to maintain that all day long?"

"It will get easier with time," Ms. Apotheker says. "You don't go into the gym on the first day and chest-press one hundred pounds. It takes hard work and practice to get there."

Considering that I'm literally pushing a boulder up a mountain, her analogy is a good one. To get results, I'll have to be patient and committed.

"I think we're done for today," Ms. Apotheker says. "Work on it every day, starting with twenty-minute sessions." She rifles through her crochet pocketbook and retrieves a business card. "Call me in a few weeks and let me know how it's going."

I slip the card inside my jean's pocket. "Thank you."

Ms. Apotheker dips a ladle into the cauldron, pours the elixir into a glass jar, and twists a lid on tight. "Put a few spoonfuls in an oil burner if you're having trouble conjuring up the vision." She holds out the jar. "If that doesn't work, swallow a tiny amount: a half of a teaspoon should be enough."

"There will be no oral consumption." Damian snatches the jar from Ms. Apotheker's grasp.

"A half of a teaspoon won't hurt–"

Damian cuts off Ms. Apotheker mid-sentence. "You cannot drink this." Damian's black eyes bore into mine. "Do you understand me?"

"Yes, your majesty, sir." My voice drips with sarcasm.

"We'll have to work on your tone, but I like the sound of that." Damian's eyes twinkle mischievously. I roll mine.

We take the elevator back down to the lobby. Ms. Apotheker walks us out and locks the school doors behind her.

"Thank you so much for everything," I tell her again. "I really appreciate it."

"Of course, my dear. We'll be in touch." She climbs inside a vehicle that looks like a Volkswagen Beetle, waves, and drives away.

"How do I get home?" I ask, still gawking at Enchantments Academy. Up in the multi-colored sky, the sun shines like a golden flame. Its rays illuminate what must be millions of crystals, each one a building block. From the exterior walls to the pathways surrounding the school, everything glistens like gems.

Part of me is sad to leave, but another part can't wait to get the hell out of here. I haven't forgotten how I was treated at the border.

"Not so fast," Damian says. "We aren't leaving yet. I want to show you the greatest wonders of Aurelia."

I can't help but grin like an idiot. None of this is a required part of his assignment. Damian's doing this for me. Then, I remember that he's a prejudiced jerk, and I'm an outsider. My smile falters. "Will I be welcome?"

Damian rests his arm over my shoulders. "You're with me. If anyone bothers you, they'll regret it." His tone takes on a hard edge. He isn't messing around. "This way." We walk along a trail that's paved with sapphires. "Our first stop is about a half mile away."

We enter a field of wildflowers: black eyed susans, orange tiger lilies, and purples lupines sway in the breeze. The air above them shimmers. "This is beaut–" I choke on the rest of the word, my heart in my throat. A tuft of orange fur pokes between a cluster of daisies. Hand to my chest, I gaze over the flowers at the animal crouched behind them. I stumble backwards. "Damian," I whisper. "We have to get out of here."

Damian furrows his brow, following my gaze. The lion leaps, claws extended. "Look out!" I shout. Damian ducks. He gets out of the way in the nick of time.

Damian faces the lion: fists up, feet wide, ready for a fight. "What's your problem, Weston?" Damian's lip curls into a sneer.

The lion snarls back. Frantic, I look around for a rock or something to throw, but come up empty. Even as my heart rattles, shaking me to the core, I step beside Damian, my fists raised. Maybe by some miracle I'll access my blue power and destroy this beast.

Damian gives me the side-eye. "What the hell are you doing?"

"Fighting," I say, sounding much more confident than I feel.

"Get out of the way. I got this," Damian says.

"Not a chance."

The lion growls. "Cut it out," Damian says. "Don't make me hurt you."

A whirlwind appears, a tornado of black dust, and the lion is replaced by a guy around Damian's age. He shakes out his dark blonde hair; it curls around his face like a lion's mane.

"Smart move, Wes," Damian says. "Looks like you know what's good for you."

"Let's be real," Wes says. "If you weren't the prince, I'd eat you for a snack." He mimes licking his finger. "I hear nightingale tastes like chicken."

Damian puffs his chest out. "I don't need to shift to fight you. Man to man, I'll crush you."

"We could schedule a duel if you'd like. Winner takes the throne," Wes says. "Aurelia is falling apart under the Nightingale's reign. The economy sucks. Terroristic threats are at an all-time high. Everyone wants your family out."

"What fake news outlet have you been watching?" Damian asks. "National support for the Nightingales is on the rise." Damian puts his hands on my back. "If that's all, we'll be on our way."

"You didn't introduce me to your friend," Weston studies me through narrowed yellow eyes. "Weston Lyon." He holds out his hand. I don't offer mine. He slowly lowers his. "And you are? I haven't seen you around before."

"None of your business," Damian says, nudging my side. "We're outta here." We walk away, leaving Weston behind us. Damian's posture is erect, hands clenched at his side.

"What was that about?" I ask.

"When the Crowes were dethroned, the royal families voted on who would take over. The Lyons lost by one. They've never gotten over it."

I remember what the soldiers said at the border: *The Lyons should've won. I swear that vote was rigged.*

"Here we are," Damian says, his arms outstretched.

Just ahead of us is the largest volcano that I've ever seen. Golden sparks emerge from the opening: some small, others large, like a fireworks show. "Wow," I say. "Where are we?"

"Mount Zamus," Damian says. "Otherwise known as where magic began." He sits on a flat rock, and motions to the space beside him. I sit, my gaze glued on the scene unfolding before me. Mount Zamus sputters: something that looks like a blue shooting star escapes. It soars across the rippling sky, past strips of orange, blue and purple magic.

"This is…" I'm speechless. There isn't a word in the English language that encapsulates the beauty of this place.

"The legend begins when a goddess and a demon fell madly in love. Their union was forbidden, but they couldn't stay away from one another. They kept their love a secret until Zamus, their first and only child was born.

"Half-god, half-demon, Zamus was considered an abomination. The council of gods concluded that because of the demon blood flowing through him, he couldn't be trusted. He was banished to a world created just for him, this place we now call Aurelia. All of his power was removed from his soul and confined to this volcano, where they rationalized that he couldn't use it to hurt anyone. He was sentenced to isolation for all of eternity.

"For thousands of years, Zamus lived in loneliness and despair. Then, he discovered a portal to earth. There, he met and fell in love with Aurelia, a human. When she reciprocated his feelings, he wanted to show her his world. The very first time she came here, the volcano erupted, drowning her in hot lava made of both demon's and god's magic.

"She should've died instantaneously. Miraculously, Aurelia survived, but she was forever changed. The power became part of her.

"Aurelia and Zamus went on to have many children who inherited their power. They created their own race: part human, part demon, and part god. Today, we call them witches. All of us are descendants of Aurelia and Zamus. Some of us may have more demon blood in us than others, but we all have the capacity for good or evil.

"And that's why they say this is where magic began. Without Aurelia and Zamus's love, none of us would be here today."

"That's incredible," I say. "What about the gods and the demons? Do they still exist?"

"Thousands of years ago, there was a bloody and brutal war between them. Most were killed. The few that survived tend to keep to themselves. They stay in their own realms, and we rarely see them. Occasionally, a god will send an angel down to check on us, but that's the extent of it."

"Come." Damian reaches for my hand. "There's someplace else I want to show you." We walk, hand-in-hand, down a trail that looks like emeralds. Every place our fingers touch sends jolts of electricity up my arm and through my heart.

Around the bend, water roars, crashing furiously. As the waterfall comes into view, my jaw falls open. It's ginormous, at least twice the size of Niagara Falls. Frothy cascades plunge over the mossy cliff, hurtling into a circular body of water. Droplets fly through the shimmery air, pelting my face, slick on my skin.

"We call it Clarity," Damian says.

"Because the water's clear?" I ask.

"Because it clears up uncertainties in your life." Damian says. "It provides clarity."

"How?" I ask. "Can I ask it a question?"

Damian shakes his head. "It doesn't work like that. After you're fully submerged, it decides what to reveal to you."

"Submerged?" I repeat.

"We're going swimming," Damian says.

I look down at my sweater, jeans and sneakers. Near the waterfall, the air is warm and thick like summer, but I'm not prepared to swim. "I didn't bring a bathing suit."

"We could go skinny dipping." Damian raises his eyebrows suggestively.

"In your dreams, maybe."

"I thought you'd say that." Damian points to a weeping willow tree. "You'll find a bathing suit and towels over there." I pause, trying to process this sudden change of plans. "Trust me, you don't want to miss this. It's one of the coolest things in Aurelia."

"Okay," I nod. "But it better not be a thong!"

The tree's branches sweep towards the ground, creating a curtain of leaves. I brush them aside and step inside the complete privacy of nature's dressing room. A blue polka dot one-piece bathing suit is folded on top of a beach towel.

I slip out of my clothes, pull on the swimsuit, and push my way back through the branches. My breath catches in my throat. In his swim trunks, it's fairly obvious that Damian is a descendant of the gods. Every part of his body has been sculpted to perfection: the swell of his biceps, the defined musculature of his back. I shake my head, and pull myself together. He's nothing but a royal jerk. I need to stop staring before he notices. If his head grows any larger, it might explode.

"You look great." Damian grins, and I feel like I might melt into a bowl of jelly. I really need to get a grip.

"Thanks. Where'd you get the suit from?"

"It's my sister's. You're about the same size. I chose that color because it matches your eyes."

Why does the fact that he knows the color of my eyes make my heart beat faster and my cheeks feel hot? I really need to get my head out of my ass. Falling for a guy like Damian would lead to nothing but heartbreak. "What now?" I ask.

"We jump in," Damian says. I follow his lead, the grass tickling my bare feet. Alongside the water, I almost slip on the mossy rocks. Damian steadies me; his hand on my back. "Ready?" He asks, black eyes twinkling.

"Um," I look down. From here, I can see the water churning, foaming from its mouth like a rabid animal. I shiver, unsure. "I don't know."

"Hold my hand," Damian says. "We'll jump together." I'm not sure if I take his hand because I need to, or because how good it felt to hold it before. "One, two, three."

We jump together. In an instant, I'm underwater, spinning round and round. I'm not sure when, but I lose Damian's hand. I'm alone, flailing, trying to swim up, but the undercurrent pulls me deeper. I open my eyes, searching for Damian, but all I see is blackness, like I'm wrapped in ink. In a panic, I scream. I choke as water enters my lungs. My legs kick. My arms reach for the surface. But it's no use. I'm drowning. This is it. This is the end. I wish that I'd made amends with Saria. I'd give anything for one last chance to tell my family that I love them.

As fast as Clarity sucked me in, it spits me out. I'm thrown to the surface, sputtering and coughing to expel the water from my lungs. Clarity, my ass. This place is a scam. The only thing that's clear to me is that I'm never coming back here again. After I catch my breath, I'm going to tell Damian off for bringing me to this wretched place.

Damian rises up from below. I stare, openmouthed. He's outlined by stars that shine like moonlight. Illuminated by celestial light, he's even more handsome. I admire his full lips, chiseled cheekbones, and angular features.

"What's happening?" I whisper. I have this urge to pull him close and never let go. He looks like an angel. Maybe I did die back there. If this is heaven, I'm not sure that I mind.

The breeze whispers: *He's made for you.*

I shake my head. No, it can't be true.

The wind whistles: *He's the one for you.*

From the look on Damian's face, he's just as stunned as I am.

Don't resist. You're meant to be together.

Tears fill my eyes, but I'm not sure why. I'm overwhelmed by so many emotions: shock, denial, disbelief, fear… And even though I don't want to admit it: joy.

Damian's hand cups my chin. Our eyes meet. I couldn't look away if I wanted to. I could stare at him until the end of time.

He leans down, and his lips touch mine. Electricity slides down my body. We kiss, again and again and again, in a frenzy, like we're crazed. Maybe we are.

His hands drift down my back, below my waist, and then they're on my bottom. He lifts me by my ass, his rock-hard abs pressed against my torso. I wrap my legs around him, digging my fingers into his hair as we kiss again.

"Damian!" An unfamiliar voice breaks the spell, and we spring apart.

"Fallon, what the hell are you doing here?" Damian groans. "I reserved this space. It's supposed to be all mine today."

"Having a private party, I see," Fallon's gaze flicks in my direction, venom evident in her tone. She tosses her long black hair over her shoulders. "Get out now. We need to talk."

"It can wait," Damian says.

"It's urgent."

"I'm busy."

"If you don't get out right now, I'm going to tell Father what I just saw," Fallon says, hands on her hips.

Damian groans and turns to me. "I'm sorry. My sister's a pain in the ass."

"It's okay," I say. "I'll get dressed while you two talk." I hoist myself out of the water and head back to the changing area. As I dry myself off and change back into my street clothes, Damian and Fallon speak in hushed, angry tones. I slip out from behind the tree, Fallon's swimsuit folded in my arms. As I walk towards them, their voices grow louder.

"Mind your business," Damian growls.

"Your decisions reflect poorly on the entire family. Royalty should not be fraternizing with filth."

"She's not filth."

"Her mother's a traitor, and she's a nimwit half-breed. Calling her filth is generous. There's a few choice words that come to mind, but as a princess, it's unbecoming for me to use that type of language."

I clear my throat. "Since I'm not a princess, I can use any language that I see fit. And right now, there's only one word coming to mind." I pointedly look Fallon up and down. "Bitch."

Fallon's cheeks turn red, her fists clenched at her sides. "You're going to let your little whore talk to me like that?"

Damian shrugs. "You deserved it. Also, she's not a whore. Now, if you don't mind, we'll be on our way."

"Not so fast." Fallon puts her hands on her hips. "Our parents are requesting your presence. Now."

Damian sighs. "I'll talk to them later. First, I have to make sure that Zoeli gets home safely."

Fallon shakes her head. "The king and queen have summoned *both* of you. You're to go to the palace immediately."

Damian's brow furrows. "Both of us?"

"Yes." Fallon's lips curve into a sinister smile. "You and your little nimwit." She cackles, her dark brown eyes boring into mine. "My father doesn't think too highly of your kind."

I glare right back at her. "I don't think too highly of bigots who think that they're better than others."

"That's the KING that you're talking about," Fallon hisses.

"Cut it out." Damian holds up one hand. "Tell them we'll be right there."

"Will do." As Fallon spins on her heel, her form fades, blending into the background. A nightingale flies overhead, soaring between ripples of green and purple magic. Then, she's gone.

"I'm sorry about Fallon. She can be... difficult."

"I noticed."

"My parents won't be unkind to you," Damian says. I wish I felt as sure about that as he sounds. "If you don't want to go, I understand. We'll just skip out of here."

"Won't you get in trouble?"

Damian shrugs. "It won't be the first time."

I shake my head. "I'll go. I want to know what they want from me."

Damian gestures down the trail. "Okay, my lady. Your chariot awaits."

Chapter Eighteen

Zoeli

At the end of the trail, the limo waits. We slide into the back. Damian opens the mini-fridge and snaps open a soda. "You want a drink?"

"Sure." The can is cold in my hands.

"To the palace, Oliver." Damian yells to the driver up front.

"Yes, sir." Oliver peels out, rubber burning as we take off. I stare out the window, people watching. Kids play hop-scotch, leaping much higher and farther than would be possible in the human realm. A mom tosses her baby in the air: the infant floats on the glittery air, a squeal of laughter before she falls back into her mother's arms. A couple sits on a park bench, holding hands, watching the colorful waves of magic reel across the sky. They kiss, his fingers tangled in her hair.

I glance over at Damian: wavy dark hair, chiseled jaw, strong arms folded across his chest. As much as I hate to admit it, part of me longs to be wrapped up in them again. The other part of me can't believe that I degraded myself by making out with someone who thinks he's better than me. I'm not going to let some stupid waterfall dictate my love life, that's for sure. "I'm still trying to process what happened at the waterfall—"

Damian puts one finger over his mouth, hushing me. "We'll talk later," he whispers, tilting his head towards the front of the limo. "Oliver reports everything back to my parents."

"Oh," I say, my hands wringing in my lap. I feel stupid and sleazy, like a dirty little secret. I'm not sure what I expected. Maybe now that we're out of the waterfall, he realizes that our make out session was a big mistake. "Won't Fallon tell them?"

Damian shakes his head. "She won't rat on me. I have too much on her."

We drive past a cluster of skyscrapers. As we emerge from their shadows, the palace comes into view. My jaw falls to the floor.

On an island all its own, perched at the very top of a small mountain, the palace rises up into the clouds. A stone bridge leads the way, its seven arches spanning a sparkling turquoise river. Intricate sculptures of animals are displayed on pillars erected along the bridge, each standing at least twenty feet tall. First, a lion, standing up on its hind legs, its mouth open in a ferocious roar. At its feet, a plaque reads, The Lyons.

Next we pass a hawk, its wings wide like it's in flight, razor-sharp talons holding a plaque that reads, The Hawkes. "These statues represent the royal families," I say, as we approach the deer. She's tall, her muscles defined, chin lifted in a regal pose, an adorable fawn by her side. "The Deeres," I read aloud.

I'm not prepared for what comes next. The statue has been so badly defaced that I can barely recognize it. The bird is decapitated, only jagged rock left where its head belongs. Its wings are covered with dents, as if someone took a sledgehammer to them over and over again. Spray-painted graffiti is everywhere, some of the words so vile that I can't bear to read them. *Traitor. Whore. Human-lover.* Tears well up in my eyes.

"I'm sorry you had to see that," Damian says.

"I didn't know they still hated us so much," I say.

"The vandalism happened a long time ago," Damian says. "The statue should've been replaced. I'll talk to my father about it."

I pretend to wipe a smudge off my sneakers, my head bowed low. I don't want to see the rest of the statues.

Once we've crossed the bridge, the limo follows a narrow, twisty path up the mountain. We speed around the curves. Even with a steep drop alongside us and no guardrail to prevent a fall, Oliver drives like a madman. I cling to the door's handle, my knuckles white.

We pull up to the palace. Oliver sprints around the side of the limo, and opens the door. I step outside, looking up in awe. It's something out of a fairytale. Ribbons of color swirl around dozens of circular stone towers, dipping and sliding over archways and stained-glass windows. One by one, colors streak across the sky, like paint strokes on a canvas. They meld together to create a man's face. I gasp. The man looks like an older version of Damian: dark hair, smoldering eyes, a strong jawline. The image hovers in the clouds, looming over the palace.

Damian barks out a laugh. "My father's always showing off. Come on, let's go in."

Two armored knights open the double doors in unison. Inside, a butler waits. "Good afternoon, Prince Damian." He bows in greeting. "The king and queen await your arrival in the great hall." A gold chandelier illuminates an enormous family portrait of the Nightingales. The king wears a stone-cold expression, his arms folded across his chest. Beautiful women stand on either side of him: his wife and daughter both looking like knock-outs. Black eyeliner makes Fallon's dark eyes pop. A body-hugging dress accentuates her curves. Queen Taya looks flawless: skin gleaming, an elegant gown draping on the floor. Damian leans against the wall, wearing a black tuxedo and his trademark lazy grin. If I didn't know better, I'd think they were a mafia family.

The butler leads us down a corridor. Every tiny detail is exquisite. Gold trim lines the floors and ceilings. Spotless marble floors shine. A maid is on her hands and knees, scrubbing some invisible imperfections. Every piece of furniture is Queen Anne style: mahogany wood, carved curlicues, plush velvet cushions.

We follow the butler through a labyrinth of cavernous hallways: turning left, then right, and then left again until I'm lost and dizzy. My heart pounds. Sweat beads along my hairline.

The butler opens an ornately carved wooden door. At the far end of the room, the king and queen sit on golden thrones. We walk down the center aisle, past rows and rows of blue velvet chairs. Damian and I sit in the front row. The king and queen are up on a low-level stage. I lift my chin to face them.

"Good afternoon." The king's voice booms, vibrating in my bones.

"Father, do we really have to meet here?" Damian asks. "Couldn't we have a charcuterie board in the living room or something?"

"I don't entertain half-breeds in my living quarters." The king waves his arm, his blue and gold cape swinging open. Underneath, he wears a blue tunic with a gold waistband.

"Keifer, enough." The queen glares at her husband. She also dons blue and gold: her long satin dress falling in waves to the floor, a golden belt cinching her waist. A lavish crown sits atop her wavy hair, its long spikes encrusted with crystals. The king wears a more traditional crown: gold with diamonds and sapphires. "It's a pleasure to meet you, Zoeli. Welcome to Nightingale Palace."

"Thank you, Queen Nightingale," I murmur, willing my voice to stop shaking.

"Call me Taya." The queen smiles. "How's your mom. She was my best friend growing up. We even went to nursing school together. I never used my nursing degree, though. After Keifer asked me to marry him, my plans changed." Taya seems wistful. I wonder if she's happy with the choices she made.

"My mom's good," I say. "She loves working in the ER."

"And your dad?" Taya asks. "Are they still madly in love?"

I think of my parents: the way my dad looks at my mom, his eyes full of adoration, how they sneak kisses in the kitchen, a passionate embrace when they think no one is watching, how they hold hands on their hikes through the woods. "Yes, very much."

"Disgusting." The king shakes his head. "Human vermin are not fit to be our mates."

"Oh, stop it." Taya pats her husband's arm. "My husband's very old-fashioned."

"I'm unfamiliar with Aurelian vernacular. Is 'old-fashioned' a euphemism for bigoted and stupid around here?" I should've bit my tongue, but I have a hard time holding back when it comes to my family. I brace myself for the consequences.

I swear the king's pupils turn red for a fraction of a second. Didn't Damian say that according to the legend, all witches are partly demon, god, and human? I wonder how genetics work when they're passed down, and if Keifer could be mostly demon. Can we choose which part we embrace? "Keifer, calm down." Taya puts her hand on his thigh. "Remember, they're teenagers. They don't think before they speak."

His fists clench and unclench. Judging by the look of this place, I'm about to be beheaded on a guillotine, or thrown in a dungeon with a fire-breathing dragon for the rest of my life. The king's lips twist into a scowl. He pats his wife's hand. "This type of uncouth behavior is what's expected from her kind."

"Let's get to the point," Damian says. "Why did you call us here?"

"It was my idea," Queen Taya says. "But it obviously isn't going as I had hoped. I wanted to meet Zoeli."

Behind the king and queen, an object glows inside a glass case. Four soldiers surround it from every angle. One has a bazooka-like weapon strapped across his chest.

"I also wanted to warn you," The queen continues. "Talon's militia has plans that target you and your sister. Every day more witches join their terror group. We're doing all we can to keep your family safe."

"Because the queen insists," King Keifer chimes in. "I say let the traitor and half-breeds fend for themselves."

"Talon wants you dead, Keifer. His ultimate goal is to be the king of Aurelia," Taya says. "He wants humans captured and brought to Aurelia as slaves. While you may not agree with marrying humans, you know it's wrong to enslave them." King Keifer doesn't respond, which makes me wonder if he does. "We're fighting on the same side," Taya continues. "We need to stick together."

"And you have a soft spot for Alaina," the king says.

"Well, yes," Taya admits. "She was my closest friend. If you won't agree to grant her a pardon, it's the least we can do."

I stare up at the display case, trying to figure out what's inside. "Admiring my scepter, I see." The king follows my gaze, his lips curving into a wild grin.

"I'm wondering what's in there that needs to be so heavily guarded. It's hard to see between the soldiers."

"It's the most powerful magical weapon in the world." The king's eyes gleam. "And it's all mine."

"Ours." Taya reminds him.

King Keifer walks to the display case, his cape trailing behind him. He motions for the guards to step aside. When he turns around, he holds up a staff-like magic wand. On its end, a crystal sphere glows. "This is the great ancestral scepter. It contains the magic of hundreds of witches."

"How?" I ask. "Was their power stolen?"

"Taken, not stolen," the king says. "When witches break magical law, the court sentences them to lose it. Forever."

Taya must notice my expression, because she smiles warmly. "Keifer, don't scare her. A sentencing so severe is very rare, and only considered when crimes are egregious. Most of the scepter's power was willingly donated by witches on their deathbeds. Think of it like an organ donation. When a witch dies, their power dies too. By giving their power, they get to live on, protecting the country that they love."

"How does all that magic fit inside that tiny space?" I ask. The sphere sparkles, waves of color emanating from it: mostly orange, yellow, and red. I remember what Ms. Apotheker said about blue power being the rarest. Something like pride wells up inside me.

The king's lips curl up in disgust. "Does this nimwit half-breed know nothing?"

"It's called zoxanite," Damian says, ignoring his father. "It's a special crystal that can hold magical power indefinitely. Zoxanite exists only on Aurelia, and it's even scarce here."

"All of the zoxanite mined in Aurelia belongs to me," the king says. I study him: his incredible height, slicked back hair, the unhinged gleam in his eyes as he points the scepter at me. I shudder. A man like that shouldn't have so much power. No man should. "I could blast you into a thousand pieces." A sly smile spreads across his face. "Lucky for you, I have another appointment to attend to." He hands the great ancestral scepter to one of his guards, and it's promptly returned to its case. "This was lovely. As this was a one-time exception," King Keifer side-eyes his wife. "I trust that we won't be seeing you again. Damian, see the nimwit out."

The king's boots clack across the marble floor. The door bangs shut. I let out a breath I didn't know I was holding. "Let's go," I say.

Taya walks us out of the great hall, and into the hallway. As we say our goodbyes, ready to head in separate directions, she takes my hand. "Can I have a moment with you, Zoeli?"

Damian faces me, his eyes inquiring. I nod. He moves out of earshot but never out of sight, leaning against the wall at the end of the hallway.

"Tell your mother that I miss her," Taya lowers her voice to a whisper. "And that I tried." Her fingers loop around mine, her grip tightening. "I did everything I could to get her pardoned, but he wouldn't hear it." She pauses. "When we got married, I wanted to make a difference. I thought I could soften his heart. I haven't failed entirely. Lord knows, things would be much worse around here if it wasn't for me." Taya shakes her head. "I'm sorry. I'm rambling now. I want Alaina to know that it wasn't my choice to stop speaking to her. He won't allow it."

"I understand," I say. It's clear to me now that Taya doesn't love her husband. Maybe she never did. She sacrificed her own happiness when she married him, hoping that she could galvanize change in Aurelia. "I'll tell her."

Taya squeezes my hand one more time, then walks away.

"I have one last thing that I want to show you before we go," Damian says.

As we navigate through long corridors: left, left, and right, the butler darts up to us, his hands waving frantically. "Prince Damian, where are you going?"

"Don't worry about it," Damian says, walking faster.

"The king hasn't given, um, permission for your guest to visit longer. He ordered that she leave the premises immediately."

"Run!" Damian takes my hand, and then we're off, sprinting, laughing wildly, the butler in our wake. Damian throws a door open, outside air whipping my face as we enter a courtyard.

Just like the rest of the palace, every element of its design is majestic: stone statues of gods and goddesses, water spraying from three-tiered opulent fountains, sparkling pavers in rich patterns on the ground.

In the center of the courtyard is a ginormous chunk of zoxanite: a boulder twice Damian's height, and longer than a semi-truck. Magic rolls from it in colorful waves, oscillating up into the sky: strips of purple, indigo, blue, yellow and green. Every color of the rainbow: dazzling, bold, stretching out into the atmosphere.

"This is where the colors come from," I say aloud. "That's why they're so much brighter here, and you can't see them from the outskirts."

"Yes. We call it the Rock of Vitality." Damian says. "This is the power source that allows for the expansion of our country. When Aurelia was first created, it was smaller than central park. Now, it's bigger than New Jersey. The most beautiful part is that it comes from all of us. Every Aurelian, past and present, in order to gain citizenship, must donate one percent of their power."

"That's amazing," I say.

"A few months after birth, there's a ceremony," Damian explains. "The infant is placed in contact with the Rock of Vitality while their family casts a spell. One percent of the baby's power is extracted and transferred into the crystal. Then and only then, are they considered a true Aurelian. It's a baptism of sorts, I suppose."

Two guards dash around a corner. One points at us. "There they are!" The guards race in our direction. "She has to go, now!

Damian holds up his hands in surrender. "We're outta here. Someone call for Oliver."

Chapter Nineteen

Zoeli

When we return to the human realm, we don't land at the portal where we entered. Even though Oliver dropped us off by the border, and we walked down the same trail, the huge tree with the "A" carved on its trunk is nowhere in sight.

"Where are we?" I ask, surveying the woods. As evening descends, the sun is a glowing orange orb and the clouds take on a purple hue, but it's nothing compared to the sky in Aurelia.

"Just a half-mile from the entry portal," Damian says. "Portals only go in one direction. It's a security measure. It prevents invaders from entering Aurelia when the portal opens on the other side. On the way in, we're careful to close the portal right behind us. Then, of course, the guards wait at the border as an extra precaution."

Damian takes a few steps, leaves crunching under his boots. He stops, swooping me into his arms. "Finally, we're alone." Before I know it, I'm up against a tree, Damian's body on mine. His hands are everywhere: in my hair, on my waist, running down my back. His lips brush against my neck, my earlobe, my cheek, and then land on my lips.

It feels like I'm under his spell. It occurs to me that I might be. It would explain why I'm having such a hard time resisting him. I'm usually stronger than this.

We kiss until I'm breathless. My body feels like it was set on fire.

"This is crazy." Damian watches me through smoldering black eyes. He sits at the base of the tree. I curl up in his arms. "I never expected this," he says.

"You're telling me," I murmur. I can't think straight. What am I doing? I can't fall in love with him.

"Did you like Aurelia?"

"Besides the fact that everyone there hates me for existing, it was pretty cool."

"When I become king, things will be different." He pauses. "I just hope I make it there."

"What do you mean? Aren't you guaranteed the position?"

"My father and I don't always get along."

"I can't imagine why," I mutter.

"Sometimes, when we fight, he threatens to accuse me of a crime so that I'm ineligible to become king. Then, assuming my sister gets married, her husband would be appointed king."

"Do you think he would really do that to you?"

"Maybe." Damian shrugs. "That's why I have to tread lightly. I have to make sure that the great ancestral scepter doesn't end up in the wrong hands."

I envision the glowing orb, vibrating with great power. "How much damage can it do? Has it been used in battle before?"

"It doesn't work like that. Once its power is unleashed, it attacks, and then it dies."

"But the zoxanite that powers Aurelia…" I pause, thinking. "That magic is used and doesn't die."

"Because it's not being used to kill or destroy," Damian explains. "When disembodied magic is used for destruction, it's a one-time deal. It's nature's way of preventing world annihilation."

The sky darkens. Shadows of trees and swaying branches elongate, shrouding half of Damian's face. A gust of cold air runs its fingers through my hair. I shiver.

"You're cold," Damian says. "We should go." Reluctantly, we unravel from our embrace. Holding hands, we follow the trail, climbing over rocks and squeezing past brush. A wolf howls.

Even though it was only this morning, it feels like it was a million years ago when we first walked this path together, on our way to Aurelia. I'm not the same person who I was a few hours ago. I'll never be that person again.

Today was the first day that I felt pure hatred. Their malice and bigotry sunk deep into my bones and will never leave me. I'll never forget the horror of that feeling: knowing that they would kill me in the blink of an eye. No mercy and no remorse because my life has no value to them.

It was also the first day that I felt like I could fall in love with Damian. I remember the feel of his lips on mine, the words Clarity whispered in the wind: *You're meant to be together*.

But how can I be with someone who doesn't respect me? As hard as it's going to be, I must resist his charms. I can't risk falling for someone who thinks that I'm less than him. True love can only exist between equals.

A few minutes later, we climb inside Damian's SUV. He turns the ignition, blasts the heat, and steps on the gas. "I hate to do this, but I'm going to have to ask you not to tell anyone about us. Not your best friend. Not even your mom. Your aunt is a big gossip. If she finds out, word will spread like wildfire."

I stare out the window into the darkness. "I understand. It's *beneath* you to date a half-breed. I wouldn't want to destroy your stellar reputation, your majesty."

"Zoeli, that's not it," Damian says, taking my hand. "I'm sorry for the ignorant things that I said about half-breeds. I could blame it on the way I was raised, but there's no excuse. I take full accountability for my words. I was wrong, and I'm sorry that I hurt you."

"I appreciate your apology." Even though he sounds genuine, I know it takes time and effort to unlearn ingrained biases. Over the long term, I hope that he shows me that he's willing to put in the work. If not, there's no hope for us to be together. "But if you're not ashamed of me, then why do I need to be so secretive?"

"If my father finds out, he'll forbid me to see you. He could even press charges against us. Under Aurelian law, it's a crime to date anyone with human blood. We'd spend the rest of our lives locked in a dungeon."

The severity of it all hits me like a freight train. I swallow hard. "If we can never be together, then why would Clarity say…" My voice trails off.

Damian parks in front of my house. His black eyes are wide like saucers: unsure, almost vulnerable. "I'm going to figure it out, Zoeli." He traces my jawbone. "I just need you to give me some time." His hands tangle in my hair. He pulls me to him, his lips brushing against mine, over and over again. I want to pull away, but I'm powerless. It feels too good.

"There's one more thing I want to ask before you go," Damian says. "Will you connect with me telepathically?" It's so absurd that I burst into laughter. I'm doubled over, trying to catch my breath. Damian watches me with that amused twinkle in his eye. "I'm happy to entertain you, but I'm not joking. My mom said that you're in danger, Zoeli. I need to be able to contact you. If you're captured, they'll take your phone."

I take a deep breath, holding back giggles. "I'm sorry. It's just that I thought you were going to ask me to go on a date or to be your girlfriend or something *normal*." I shake my head. "I guess I should've realized by now that normal doesn't apply to us. What's this whole telepathic connection thing about? Will you be able to read my thoughts? I'm not sure how I feel about that."

"Only if you want me to. Instead of speaking aloud, you can talk to me in your head. We can contact each other from opposite ends of the world, even from different worlds. If you need me, I'll be there."

"While I appreciate your heroic intentions, you seem to forget that I have blue power and you have purple. If you're in trouble, I'll come rescue you."

"We'll see about that." He kisses my forehead, his finger trailing down the back of my neck. Goosebumps erupt on my arms. "I have to be upfront with you. Telepathic connection is meant to be for life. It can only be broken if one of us dies, or through a painful reversal process.

"Also, you can't be connected to more than one person at a time. As long as you're connected to me, you won't be able to use telepathy with anyone else."

I bite my lip, considering. Queen Taya did say that Talon's militia is targeting me. Being able to contact Damian could save my life. Still, the permanency of the decision makes me take pause. "What happens if we want to end it?"

"We can," Damian says. "I just want you to know that it will hurt."

"I'm not scared of pain," I say. Besides, after that moment under the waterfall, I *knew* that Damian and I would be inextricably linked for life– whether we're together or not. "Okay," I say. "I'll do it."

"It might not even work because, you know, you're part human," Damian says. I'm glad that he didn't say half-breed. If he did, I would've taken the deal right off the table. "Are you ready?"

"Right now?" I ask.

"I want to know that you're safe." Damian pauses. "But I understand if you need more time to think about it."

"It's okay. I'm ready." I'm determined to prove that I can do anything a full-blooded witch can. If I could complete an evulsion, why not this?

Damian leans forward until our foreheads touch. "Close your eyes. Imagine that you're opening up for me, and I'm entering you."

"Mmmm," I murmur. "I like when you talk dirty to me."

"Get your mind out of the gutter!" Damian licks his lips. "We'll have plenty of time for that later." Heat pools in my lower body. "Repeat after me." Damian's voice is soft and husky. "I open my heart. I open my mind."

"I open my heart. I open my mind." I envision my head splitting open, making space for Damian to become part of me.

"Now we are intertwined."

"Now we are intertwined." It hits me like a tidal wave, an explosion inside my eardrums. It feels like my skull's been blown to pieces. I scream, curling up into the fetal position, palms against my ears. A moment later, it stops. "Is it over?" I ask, touching my head, surprised to find that it's intact. "Did it work?"

Can you hear me? Damian's voice booms inside my head. I scream again. **Sorry. Is that better?** His voice is softer now. I nod.

"How did you do that?" I ask.

It's just like talking, but with your mind. We can also send pictures. An image of a heart appears in my mind's eye, and I smile.

Cute. "Did it work?" I ask aloud.

"Not as cute as you." Damian takes my hand, rubbing my palm with his thumb. "I should get back to the palace. My parents are hosting another stupid dinner, and I'm expected to be there."

Goodbye, Damian.

Until next time, beautiful.

***

A few hours later, I'm curled up in bed, Batman at my feet, when the voice comes out of nowhere.

I have one more question. I jolt up, scanning my empty bedroom, and then chuckle to myself. It's going to take some time to get used to this. **I've been thinking about it all night.**

Oh, God. What now?

Will you be my girlfriend?

I should just say no. Yes, our make out session was hot, but that's not a reason to jump into a relationship. *I don't want to rush into anything because of what a waterfall said.*

This isn't just about what happened under the waterfall. When I'm with you, I don't want to leave. As soon as we're apart, I'm thinking about the next time that we'll be together. The more I get to know you, the more I like you. You're smart, beautiful and a little sassy, but I like that too.

You're a good talker. I'll give you that.

What I'm trying to say is that I like you. A lot. And I know that you feel the same way about me. I could feel it in your kiss.

You're quite sure of yourself.

Am I wrong?

I sigh. I hate to admit it, but he's wearing me down. *You're not wrong, but I have some reservations. For one, you hold deep-rooted prejudices against humans. Two, you're awfully full of yourself. And three, it's not even legal for us to be together.*

I told you that I'm going to work on all of that, and I mean it. Let me prove it to you. I want to be with you, Zoe. You make me want to be a better man.

My heart melts into a puddle. I might be a fool, but at least I'll be a fool with a smoking hot boyfriend. *The guys from Club Ice are going to be disappointed when they find out I'm off the market.*

Is that a yes?

It's a yes.

I can feel his smile, like warmth inside my soul.

Chapter Twenty

Saria
One Month Later

I'm inside a bathroom stall when I overhear a conversation at the mirror.

"What are you smiling about?" I recognize Keisha's voice. "You look like a little kid at Disney World."

"Is it that obvious?" Through cracks between the stalls, I see Mallory applying lip gloss. "Last night was the best night of my life. I'm still basking in the afterglow."

"Spill the tea," Keisha says. "I want all the details."

"Let's just say that Chad's talents extend beyond the football field."

"Chad?" Keisha pauses. "You don't mean Saria's Chad?"

"Saria let herself go. Chad doesn't even like her anymore. He wants to break up with her, but he feels bad for her."

"That doesn't make it okay for you to sleep with him! Either you tell Saria or I will."

I flush the toilet, and thrust open the stall door. It crashes into the wall, creating a clamor. "Thanks, Keisha, but it looks like you're off the hook." Mallory turns around, her hand over her mouth. I lunge forward and grab a chunk of her auburn hair. "You're supposed to be my friend!"

"Ouch!" Mallory howls. "Ow, ow, ow! Let go!"

I twist and yank. As each root separates from Mallory's scalp, I separate too, severing ties from my old phony life. But there's one last thing I have to do.

I throw the clump of hair on the floor, and slam the door behind me. I stomp down the hallway. Chad stacks books in his locker.

"You're cheating on me?"

Chad's eyes widen: a deer caught in headlights. "Um, I mean, I'm sorry. I was going to tell you."

"You don't love me anymore?"

"Um, I mean, um, we've had a lot of good times together." He doesn't love me. He never did. But I can't be mad at him.

"I'm sorry," I whisper. Chad frowns, confusion in his eyes. He'll never understand what I did to him. I wasted his time. I tricked him, used him, and made him think he felt something that he never did. "I hope you're happy with Mallory. Goodbye, Chad." I walk away.

***

After school, I yell at my plant. "You're pathetic and ugly! No wonder your boyfriend cheated on you!" I'm not even lying. The plant looks half-dead. Instead of standing tall, her limp leaves hang over the edge of the pot. If she had a boyfriend, he'd probably cheat.

My phone dings. I open the group chat with Giselle, Keisha and Penny.

Giselle: Keisha told us what happened. We're on our way over.
Penny: We're taking you out tonight, and we're going to have fun!
Keisha: Forget Chad and Mallory. They deserve each other.

Less than ten minutes later, my friends burst through my front door. Penny hugs me tight. "I'm done with Mallory. I'll never speak to her again."

"Me either," Keisha says, joining the hug. "In the long run, she did you a favor. You're better off without that tool bag."

Giselle holds up a suitcase. "I brought my glam bag: makeup, hair products, and the cutest outfits I own. Forget sobbing over ice cream. Let's glam you up, go out and dance with hot guys!"

I grin. "Sounds like a plan."

An hour later, beachy waves cascade down my back. Navy eyeliner brings out the color of my eyes. "Giselle, you're a miracle worker."

"Hardly. You're naturally gorgeous. I barely did anything." She lifts a handful of dresses from her bag. "Now it's time for wardrobe." She holds up a blue tube dress in one hand and a red halter dress in the other.

"Ohhh!" Penny squeals. "The blue one is gorgeous."

"Royal blue makes red hair pop. You'll look amazing in it." I grab the dress and pass it to Penny.

"No, no." Penny hands it back to me. "It matches your eyes. It's perfect for you."

"Penny," I pause, unsure how to word this. It seems like our friendship fell into a toxic pattern that even losing my powers didn't break. "You don't have to give everything to me. If you like the dress, it's yours."

Penny stares at the dress, considering. "Okay, next time, but tonight is all about you. You're going through a break up. Now put on the dress!"

"Okay," I concede. Penny chooses a black dress with a more modest neckline. Maybe she felt uncomfortable showing too much skin.

At Club Ice, my friends and I tear up the dance floor. Giselle looks like a model, her tall slender frame accentuated by her red halter dress. Keisha's stunning in skinny jeans and a gold sequin top, her curls bouncing as she dances. Guys who offer to buy them drinks mostly ignore me.

Without my magic, I'm uncoordinated and lack rhythm. Most of my makeup is gone, a consequence of my overactive sweat glands. But none of that matters. The right guy will love me exactly as I am.

And tonight, it isn't about guys. I'm out with my best friends: my real friends. I'm my true self, and we're having a blast. It doesn't get any better than this.

A chill shakes me to the core. The hairs on the back of my neck stand up. Someone's watching me. I feel eyes all over me, like icicles sliding over my skin. I spin around, searching in every direction.

His platinum hair stands out in the crowd. He stands against the bar, his silver eyes piercing mine. When I catch his gaze, he lifts his glass, a smug look on his face. He wears a tight-black t-shirt, showcasing his biceps. Is that a tattoo? It looks like… a crown.

I touch the crown on the back of my neck, realization dawning on me. He's a royal. I can't be sure if he's a friend or enemy.

Someone touches my shoulder, and I whirl around. Penny's eyes are wide with concern. "Are you okay?"

"Oh, um." I glance over my shoulder. He's gone. "I'm just getting tired." I force a smile. "Maybe we should go home."

***

The following afternoon, Logan and I sit on his bedroom floor, comparing our plants. Logan's plant has grown since I last saw it. Bright green leaves stretch towards the ceiling. In comparison, my plant looks like it's withering away. Its leaves are brown and wilted, drooping like a frown toward the ground.

"What happened?" I ask. "I followed the care instructions. I watered it the right amount, and made sure it got sunlight."

"Did you bully it?"

"Every day. Just like you said. I called it all the horrible things I thought about myself."

"I did the opposite."

"What do you mean?"

"I told it all about you. Every wonderful thing." Logan's hazel eyes meet mine. "I told it about your adventurous spirit, and the way you know thousands of random facts about birds. I said that you have no idea how beautiful you are. Even without your magic, your smile lights up a room. I listed all the things I love about you: your sense of humor, your competitive spirit, that you aren't afraid to get dirty, how in touch with nature you are. I said that your boyfriend is the luckiest guy in the world."

"I don't have a boyfriend."

"You don't?"

"We broke up. He cheated on me."

Logan fidgets with the strings on his hoodie. "Oh, I'm sorry to hear that."

I shake my head. "No, you're not."

"You're right. I'm not. He wasn't right for–"

I kiss him before he can finish his sentence. When our lips touch, warmth flows through me. We kiss again. And again.

Magic isn't just what's born inside witches. Words are magic. They can inspire growth or cause death. Love is magic. I couldn't love someone else when I didn't even love myself.

I'm here right now, in this moment with Logan's lips on mine. I'm finally who I want to be. I'm finally where I want to be.

This is what real magic feels like. For me, this is where magic begins.

Chapter Twenty-One

Zoeli

"Watch this." I hold up my wrist so that my boyfriend can see my magical caliper. In my mind's eye, I sprint up the mountain, rolling the boulder like it's a beach ball. The numbers on my caliper take a nosedive: 1000, 500, 200, 0.

"Wow," Damian says. "That's awesome."

I smile. "I've been practicing. I still haven't figured out how to access my blue power, but I'll keep trying."

Damian lays on a checkered blanket, the breeze ruffling his hair, sunlight dancing on his skin. Over the past month, we've met at this spot at least a dozen times. Deep in the forest, we don't have to worry about anyone catching us together.

He pulls me on top of him, his hand cupping my chin. His thumb strokes the curve of my jaw. "I'm amazed by you: your strength, your perseverance, your power." My heart hammers in my chest. Is he going to say the "L" word? "You have more heart and talent than any full-blooded witch I've ever met. I'm disgusted by the way I used to think. I know I've told you before, but I want to say it again. I'm so sorry."

"I appreciate your apology," I say. "And I see your growth."

"When I'm king, I'm going to change Aurelian law. Witches with human blood will be given the opportunity to become citizens and attend the academy."

"What about humans?"

Damian pauses. "Humans don't want to coexist peacefully with witches. Witch hunters dedicate their whole lives to finding and killing us."

"Not all humans are witch hunters. It isn't fair to characterize an entire group based on the actions of a few radicalists."

"They would have to be thoroughly vetted before we allowed them in."

I nod. "That's fair."

"It's all wishful thinking.." Damian lowers his head. "Even the king doesn't have absolute power. The royals vote on any major changes to our constitution. I'm not sure how many of the old-timers will vote in favor of allowing humans in Aurelia. Most of them will still be around when I'm crowned."

"When will that be?" I ask. "After your father dies?"

"The eldest son takes the crown on his twenty-fifth birthday. So in a little over eight years, I'll be the king."

"Why twenty-five?"

"It's what the founders of Aurelia decided. It's old enough to have the maturity and experience needed for the job, but still be able to relate to the younger generation and be open to change. By ensuring that no king stays in power for too long, it helps prevent stagnation. Old kings tend to get stuck in their ways."

"Do you think you'll be ready for all that responsibility?" I ask.

"I think so. I've been preparing for it my entire life. I just hope that I don't come in during a war. Talon's militia's planning to attack. We just don't know when or where. He's emboldened by his growing numbers, so it could be any day now."

"Why are more witches joining his group? What could he possibly have to offer them?"

"There's always been fringe groups who are driven by power and hate. When your great-uncle Talon was asked to leave the palace, he rose up as a leader of a radical terror group. At that time, they were living in Aurelia, and planning a domestic attack. Luckily, our intelligence agency uncovered their plan and thwarted their attack. When the police went to arrest them, most of them were already gone. They escaped to the human realm and changed their identities. Licinia's great niece was one of them. No one ever saw her again. Who knows how many children she has by now? All of them are undoubtedly growing up on a training camp, preparing for war.

"In the years since, many more fugitives have escaped Aurelia before going to trial. They have various reasons for joining Talon's hate group: they have nowhere to go, they're angry, they have an ax to grind with Aurelia."

"What's their end goal?" I ask.

"Take over Aurelia, overthrow the Nightingale reign, and make it legal to own human slaves. There won't be a free human left if it's up to them."

"My dad…" My voice trails off.

Damian holds me tighter. "Don't worry. It's never going to happen. I won't let it." His lips linger on mine, kissing me again and again. I writhe against him, heat rushing between my thighs. His hand slides under my shirt. I kiss him harder. I'm hot, breathless.

His fingers graze the inside of my jeans. "If you want me to stop, you're going to have to tell me."

"No," I say. "Don't stop."

A few hours later, we're tangled up in the grass, moonlight shining on us. "It's getting late," Damian says.

I check my watch. "Hours feel like minutes when I'm with you," I say, pulling my shirt over my head. "Will I see you tomorrow?"

"Unfortunately, no," Damian says. "I have to go to this stupid ball at the palace." Damian grunts. "I have to get all dressed up and schmooze with the Aurelian elite."

"That doesn't sound too terrible," I say. I imagine myself in a beautiful ball gown, hoop skirt billowing, Damian twirling me across the dance floor.

"Now that looks like a good time," Damian says. As we grow closer, I find myself sharing more and more with him without meaning to.

I flush. "That wasn't meant for you." I slip my sneakers on. "But I do wish that I could go."

"Me too," Damian says, pulling me close. I rest my head on his chest, his breath in my hair. "Me too."

***

Two mornings later, I'm hunched over the kitchen table, doing algebra homework. The doorbell rings. I hear Mom's footsteps, clattering down the stairs. The front door swings open.

"Alaina, we have the most incredible news! We had to tell you in person!" I recognize Aunt Gwenna's voice. "This is my daughter. Cali, meet your Aunt Alaina."

"Caliah!" Mom says. "The last time I saw you, you were just a baby. Come in, come in. I'll make us some tea."

My fingers clamp around my pencil. I've heard of her, but I've never met my cousin. As their voices grow louder, I smooth my hair and rumpled t-shirt.

"Zoeli," Mom says, entering the room. "This is your cousin, Cali. What a brilliant surprise!"

Caliah holds out her hand, her turquoise eyes shining. Strawberry-blonde curls frame her flawless face: immaculate skin, endless eyelashes, a tiny nose, pouty lips. She moves gracefully, her lithe body clothed in designer fashion. I feel like an oaf next to her. "It's a pleasure to meet you, Zoeli," she says.

I shake her hand. "Likewise."

Saria walks in, yawning as she pulls out a chair. "What's going on?"

"Saria, meet Caliah," Mom says.

"Everyone sit down," Aunt Gwenna orders. "We have big news that's going to impact this family for centuries to come."

Mom turns on the tea kettle while everyone settles around the kitchen table. Aunt Gwenna waits for all eyes to be on her.

"What is it?" Mom asks. "We're all in suspense."

"Caliah, here," Aunt Gwenna puts her hand on her daughter's shoulder, "is going to be the queen of Aurelia."

"Excuse me?" Mom says.

My brow furrows in confusion.

"Let me start at the beginning," Aunt Gwenna says. "Queen Taya always felt that Alaina's punishment was too harsh. When she became queen, she hoped that she could convince the king to allow Alaina to return to Aurelia. She also wanted to lift the curse that took away your power to shift into a crow."

"Yes," Mom says. "Zoeli shared that with me. I was very touched."

Aunt Gwenna looks annoyed that Mom interrupted. She clears her throat. "If your mother's power is reinstated, both of you nimwits could also fly as crows, since the curse applies to Alaina and her offspring."

Saria seems to perk up. She leans forward, her legs bouncing under the table.

"But no matter how Taya tried, she could not persuade her husband. The king and queen must both agree for a pardon to be issued." Aunt Gwenna pauses, her gaze moving from one of us to the next, making sure that she has our rapt attention. "After a few conversations with Taya, I started brainstorming. Since we shared a similar goal of helping my dear sister—"

"You mean weaseling your way back into the palace." Mom cuts in.

My aunt waves her hand. "Semantics. As long as the outcome's the same, what's wrong if I benefit as well?" She raises one eyebrow. "Anyways, I started thinking about it. The Prince of Aurelia and Caliah have known each other since preschool. They've always fancied each other, but neither pursued it because they knew their relationship would be forbidden."

"Why?" Saria asks. I'm wondering the same thing, but I'm too stunned to speak.

"Because she's a Crowe and he's a Nightingale."

"So?" Saria looks puzzled.

"Because they're different species, you nimwit!" Aunt Gwenna throws her hands in the air. "Do you know nothing? Species have been forbidden to intermix ever since the Lyon and Hawke debacle."

"What debacle?" I ask. Why didn't Damian tell me about this? I'm only sixteen, so it's not like we're ready to plan a family or anything, but still…

Aunt Gwenna releases an exaggerated sigh. "Years ago, a Lyon married a Hawke. They had this grand idea that when their child shifted, it would become some kind of winged sphinx. Unfortunately, that wasn't the case. After at least twenty miscarriages, a daughter was finally born. She was healthy, beautiful and smart. All seemed well until her first shift. She was a mangled mess: organs and limbs all haphazardly pieced together. She died. It was a tragedy."

"That's horrible. How old was she?" Saria asks.

"I think around nine or ten. That's when shifting power usually comes in."

"I was seven the first time I shifted," Caliah says.

"Well, you were always advanced for your age." Aunt Gwenna beams. "You're a very gifted witch. Anyhow, I've gone off on a tangent. Where was I?" She drums her fingers on the table. "Oh, yes, so I was talking to the queen, and I asked if she had anyone in mind for her son to marry. She said some mumbo jumbo about letting Damian marry whoever he chooses, blah, blah, blah. Then I mentioned, as if it had just occurred to me, that if Damian took Caliah as his wife, Alaina could be pardoned. Oh, how wonderful it would be to see

Alaina again! We could fly together through the colorful skies of Aurelia!

"I could tell that I piqued her interest, but there was still the problem of intermixing species. Out of all of the species, the crow and the nightingale are the closest relatives. For a long time, scientists suspected that they could mate without a problem, but it remained banned out of an abundance of caution.

"After my little proposition, Taya reached out to Dr. Finkelson, a brilliant geneticist. She asked him to investigate. After studying genetic samples from both Damian and Caliah, Dr. Finkelson's expert opinion is that their DNA is compatible. He predicts that they will create a hybrid species with characteristics of both birds."

"Genetic samples?" I echo. The world seems to move in slow motion. This can't be real. I must be having a nightmare. I pinch my thigh. I bite the inside of my cheek. I can't seem to wake up.

"Yes, they both had blood drawn and swabs of cells taken from their cheeks," Aunt Gwenna says. "Dr. Finkelson thinks their child will be larger than a nightingale but smaller than a crow. The Nightingale men have always been insecure about their species' size. Once King Keifer heard 'bigger,' he was sold."

"The king announced the big news last night at the ball." Caliah pulls her phone out of her pocket. "It was the best night of my life," Caliah gushes, holding up her phone. On the screen, Caliah looks like a Disney princess. She wears a royal blue ball gown, her hair swept into a glamorous updo, wispy tendrils framing her perfect face. She dances close with

Damian, his eyes twinkling in the way I thought was only for me.

"Oh, he's handsome!" Saria says. "Congratulations!"

"I feel like the luckiest girl in the world." Caliah twirls a strawberry curl around her finger. "I've had a crush on him forever, but I never thought we'd be more than friends." I think I'm going to be sick. My stomach roils.

"This is so exciting," Saria says. "When do you think the curse will be lifted? I can't wait to fly with the crows."

"Oh, I won't be queen for eight years." Caliah holds her hand to her chest, staring adoringly at her picture of **my** boyfriend. "But I want to marry Damian way before then."

Excuse me, **ex**-boyfriend. I'm going to tear him a new one, and then dump his ass.

"Of course. We'll plan the wedding as soon as you're both eighteen." Aunt Gwenna places her hand atop her daughter's. "Secure that bag and lock it up."

I can't take it anymore. I slam my algebra book shut, and hold it to my chest. "Congratulations, Cali. It was a pleasure meeting you, but I have a lot of homework to do." I flee from the room.

I dart up the stairs and into my bedroom. The world feels like it's collapsing around me. This can't be true. Please, Damian, tell me that this isn't true.

What's wrong? Damian's voice booms inside my head. I hadn't meant for him to hear that, but I'm going to have to face this sooner or later.

What the hell happened last night?

The long pause tells me everything that I need to know.

What do you mean?

Don't play dumb. Caliah's here.

Zoe, we need to talk in person.

Did you or did you not agree to marry Caliah?

It isn't that simple.

It seems pretty simple to me. Yes or no?

Yes, but—

There's no buts! You're marrying my cousin!

I didn't even know if it was going to happen. The DNA test, the contract... It all happened months ago. Before I met you.

You didn't think that you should tell me about this? Before you slept with me?

I'm sorry. I was hoping that it wouldn't work out, that the DNA results would be incompatible and you'd never have to know.

So you're a liar!

I didn't lie to you.

A lie of omission is still a lie! I needed to know about this.

You're right. I messed up, but I'm going to fix it. I just need some time to figure it out.

How long do you think I'm going to wait around? Until after you marry Caliah and fix Aurelia? Did you expect me to be your mistress? Your dirty little secret?

Of course not, but it's complicated. My parents are so gung-ho about this marriage. I'm not sure how to tell them that I don't want this anymore. I can't exactly tell them that I've fallen in love with someone else. It's a crime to date

anyone with human blood. They could have me arrested. And my father still holds the whole Licinia thing over my head. If my relationship with her was publicized, I'd face multiple charges. Not only would I be ineligible to become king, I'd be banished from Aurelia. The great ancestral scepter, a tool that could be used for mass destruction, could end up in anyone's hands. My sister doesn't have the best taste in men. She could marry someone like my father, or worse. Aurelia will be doomed.

I swallow hard, reality hitting me like a bullet to my heart. Without me in the picture, Damian and Caliah get married and live happily ever after. They'll make positive changes in Aurelia. They'll rewrite the laws that deny rights to witches with mixed blood. Mom can visit her homeland, and reconnect with estranged friends and family. Saria will fly as a crow for the first time, a birthright that was wrongfully stolen from her.

If Damian chooses me, he'll rot in jail and Aurelia will go up in flames. It's a no-brainer.

I wish you told me before I fell in love with you.

Believe me, I never expected this to happen. We're going to make it work. I promise you.

Marry Caliah. Forget about me.

I can't do that. Zoeli, I love you.

Tears slide down my cheeks.

Goodbye, Damian.

Chapter Twenty-Two

As mom, Aunt Gwenna and Caliah ohh and ahh over pictures of wedding dresses, I slip out of the kitchen. At the top of the stairs, I tap on Zoeli's bedroom door.

When she excused herself from the kitchen, I could tell that something was wrong. I knock again, louder this time. "Zoe?" She doesn't respond.

I push the door open slowly. "Zoe?" My sister is curled up in a ball on her bed, her face pressed against her knees. "Are you okay?"

Zoeli sits up, wiping her eyes. "I'm fine." Her face is red and splotchy. I know she's been crying.

I sit at the end of her bed. "What's wrong?"

"Why do you care?"

"Because I care about you, Zoe. You're my sister. My twin sister." I've been wanting to make amends for a while, but fear of rejection held me back. "I want to apologize. I'm sorry. I never should've dated Chad, knowing what he did to you."

Zoe shrugs. "It's fine. I'm over it."

"I'm not," I say. "I'm ashamed of what I did and why I did it. I was jealous of you, Zoe. You had everything that I wanted. Chad was the only thing that you wanted that I could have."

My sister raises her eyebrows. "Jealous of me? You're the one who had everything. I couldn't set a spell to save my life."

"Maybe, but everything you had was real. You have real friends and talents. I was just a phony. It ate me up inside."

"I never knew," Zoeli says.

"I did a good job of hiding it."

"It's my turn to apologize. I'm sorry for stealing your powers."

"Don't be. It's the best thing that ever happened to me. I'm finally learning who I am."

"It was still wrong," Zoe says.

I put my hand on her arm. "I want to get back to how it used to be, when we were best friends. I miss that."

"I miss that, too."

"I know it's not going to happen overnight, but I think that over time, I can earn your trust." Zoe throws her arms around me. I hug her tight, tears streaming down both of our faces. "I love you."

"I love you." We hold each other for a few minutes.

"What's wrong, Zoe? I know you're not okay."

"I don't want to talk about it."

"Okay, but let me be there for you. What are you doing tonight? Can we watch funny movies and eat yummy snacks?"

"I can't tonight. The Exiled Crows are performing at the Battle of the Bands."

"The Exiled Crows?"

"My band," Zoe says.

"Cool name." I grin. "I wonder who came up with that."

Zoe smiles back. "I did, but my friends love it. They think it sounds cool." She takes a deep breath and smooths her hair. "I need to get it together. My friends are depending on me."

"Can I go with you? I'd love to cheer you on."

"Sure, that sounds great."

***

The announcer's voice booms through the speakers. "With Yazmin Hamdan on vocals, Zoeli McKinney-Crowe on guitar, Justin Hernandez on bass guitar, and Scott Mahoney on the drums, let's give a warm welcome to our next band, The Exiled Crows!"

My sister takes the stage, looking hot as hell in a black leather mini-dress and thigh-high purple boots. "Woohoo!" I shout and whistle.

Scott claps his drumsticks together. "One, two, three!" The Exiled Crows begin to play. As Zoe sways with the rhythm, her fingers glide across the guitar. She was born for this. The instruments meld together into an enchanting melody. Yazmin's voice is smooth as silk, her emotions palpable as she throws her head back, microphone to her lips. The audience dances, their hands in the air. My sister is a rock star.

Come to the parking lot.

I don't know where the voice comes from or why I'm compelled to follow it. I push through the crowd, making my way towards the exit. I'm in a dream, floating.

Outside, a cool breeze ruffles my hair. The streetlights look like stars, beams of golden light stretching in all directions, obscuring rows of cars. My vision blurs, like I'm underwater. In the back corner of the lot, a red expensive-looking car stands out, clear as day in the murky sea.

Walk to red Rolls-Royce

My limbs act of their own volition, gliding across the pavement. The Rolls-Royce's trunk is wide open.

Get in

I climb inside the trunk, curling up in the fetal position to fit. It slams shut above me, leaving me in total blackness.

Chapter Twenty-Three

Zoeli

As soon as The Exiled Crows leave the stage, we huddle together, jumping up and down and giving high-fives. "That was awesome!" Justin says, spinning Yazmin around.

"We tore this place up!" Scott grins.

"Hell yeah!" My heart is still racing out of control.

"Let's get drinks and watch the rest of the bands," Yazmin says.

We step into the audience. Random strangers pat me on the back or give thumbs up as I pass. I scan the crowd for Saria. She was in the front row when we got on stage, but I don't see her now.

Someone taps me on the shoulder. I spin around. Damian towers over me, his black eyes wide and uncertain, searching mine. "What're you doing here?" I ask.

"I couldn't miss your show. You were amazing up there." His voice softens. "I can't lose you. Can we talk?"

"I need to find my sister," I say, slipping my phone out of my boot. A wolf appears on my screen, her teeth bared. "Licinia," I say, my blood running cold.

I have your sister. We're at the portal entrance. Come now, if you want to see her alive.

I hold my phone up so Damian can read the text message. "Let's go," he says, anger flashing in his eyes.

From there, everything's a blur. I barely remember pushing through the crowd, sprinting toward the exit and climbing into Damian's SUV. He peels out of the parking lot, my ribs slamming into the door panel as we turn hard onto the main road.

"I'm calling home," Damian says. "We need their help." He scrolls through his phone and taps a button. Ringing comes through the speakers.

"On speaker?" I ask.

"No more secrets," Damian says.

"Hello," Taya answers the call.

"Mom, there's a problem. Licinia kidnapped Saria. They're at the portal entrance. Zoeli and I are on our way. I don't know who or what we're going to find when we get there."

"I'll contact the royal guard. We may have to deploy our military depending how many they have."

"Taya!" King Keifer's voice bellows in the background. "What are you talking about?"

"Saria was kidnapped. We need to send help."

"That nimwit half-breed isn't my concern."

"Keifer, your son is on his way over there!"

"If that idiot wants to put himself in harm's way, that's his problem."

"They're at the portal entrance. They're trying to invade Aurelia. We have to do something." Taya says. "Damian, let me go talk some sense into your father. Take care of yourself and Zoeli. We'll be there soon." The call disconnects.

"Do you think they'll come through?" I ask.

"I think so," Damian says. "Father can be stubborn, but I don't think he'd let me fight alone."

We turn onto bumpy, unpaved trails, but Damian isn't slowing down. Speeding through the forest, tree branches scratch the sides of the SUV like claws. We jerk to a stop. "We're here," Damian says. "You ready?"

Even though I'm terrified, I nod. The only thing I can think of is Saria. What are they doing to her? Is she okay? It's my fault that she's helpless. Maybe if I hadn't stolen her powers, she wouldn't have been captured in the first place. I have to save her.

When Damian turns out his headlights, we're submerged in blackness. I can't see my feet when they hit the ground. Damian takes my hand, and we're off, racing into the thicket. I stumble over rocks and fallen branches, feeling my way through the darkness.

As we get closer, we hear voices. A fire flickers, lighting our way. We crouch behind a bush, surveying the scene. At the portal entrance, Saria is bound to the big tree, the carved "A" just above her head. Thick rope is wrapped around Saria at least a dozen times, spanning from her shoulders to her knees. She thrashes against her restraints, but they don't budge.

At least a dozen of Talon's soldiers linger nearby, clad in combat boots and army fatigues. Flashes of movement between trees indicate that there are more. Maybe many more.

A hand clamps over my mouth. "I've got her." A gruff male voice says. There's rustling, footsteps, and then multiple hands are on me. Someone pins my hands behind my back. Fingers dig into my waist. I kick and flail, but they're stronger than me. I can't break free.

Chapter Twenty-Four

Two soldiers emerge from the darkness, one on either side of Zoeli, forcing her forward. One yanks a fistful of her hair, jerking Zoe's neck back.

"Zoe!" I lurch against the ropes, but it's no use. Tree bark scratches my back. Rope rubs and burns my skin.

Behind Zoe, four soldiers struggle with an enormous guy. "I don't think you know who you're messing with." The guy shouts, black hair falling over his eyes. "I'm Damian, the Prince of Aurelia, and you're going to pay for this!"

"We know exactly who you are." A soldier snickers, tightening his grip on Damian's forearm. Damian jerks forward, and elbows him in the side. The soldier howls and lets go. Damian swings his free arm, clocking a soldier in the jaw. The soldier drops to the ground, releasing Damian's other arm.

He throws punches, fire erupting from his fists like blowtorches. A soldier drops to the ground, hands on his face, protecting his blistering skin. Two soldiers jump Damian from behind, knocking him to the ground. They grapple in the dirt. Damian puts one in a chokehold.

"Attention!" A female voice rises above the chaos. Everyone stops what they're doing and turns towards her. The woman is strikingly beautiful: long platinum hair and smoldering black eyes. A black bodysuit clings to her petite frame. She's tiny, but oozes power. I can't take my eyes off of her. "Hello, Damian." She smiles, exposing her fangs. I shake uncontrollably, rough rope chafing my skin. This isn't real. This can't be real. "I have a favor to ask of you. I need you to open up the portal." She gestures to the ground by my feet.

Damian stares at her, unblinking. "Bitch, are you out of your mind?"

"I thought you might need a little…convincing." The vampire slinks over to Zoeli. She slips a long silver dagger out from behind her belt. Zoeli jolts back, but the guards hold her in place, her arms twisted behind her back. "Maybe this will help change your mind." The vampire presses the dagger against Zoeli's throat.

"Stop!" I yell, thrashing wildly against the ropes.

Damian clenches and unclenches his fists. "Get away from her, or I'll kill you."

The vampire cackles. She digs the dagger's point into Zoeli's neck. Rivulets of blood trickle down the blade, pooling over Zoeli's collarbone. "How about now?" The vampire asks. "One more inch and she's dead."

"Stop. Licinia, don't do this, please," Damian says.

"Open the portal."

Damian glares at her.

"Now," Licinia says. "Or I'll cut her throat."

Damian lowers his head, resigned. He kneels beside the tree I'm tied to. Using his pointer finger, he draws symbols in the dirt.

"No!" Zoeli shouts. "Don't do it, Damian!" But Damian keeps on going.

Chapter Twenty-Five

Zoeli

"No!" I yell, watching Damian's finger move on the ground over the portal entrance. I can't let this happen. I have to *do* something. I fling all the power I can muster at Licinia, but she blocks it easily. She's so much stronger than me.

A crow lands beside Licinia. In an explosion of gray smoke, the crow vanishes and re-materializes as a man. His thick gray hair blows back with the wind. He studies me with eyes that remind me of Aunt Gwenna. His claw-like finger strokes my cheek. I cringe. "Ah, my grand-niece Zoeli. I had it all before your mother married that vermin human. When I'm the king of Aurelia, you'll be my personal slave. You'll scrub my toilet until it shines like a nimwit half-breed should."

I grimace and close my eyes. Magic surges beneath my skin, flowing free and fast. In my mind's eyes, I see my magic in boulder-form, shooting like a comet. Yellow and orange power flares like a fireball, but the blue power remains inside, compact and contained. I can't let Damian open the portal. I have to save the land that Damian loves, my mother's homeland, from this sick, evil bastard.

I tug at my core with a desperation like never before. Something bursts inside me. The blue nucleus swirls, opening up, seeping into the outer layers. "Uncle Talon." My eyes spring open. "You messed with the wrong nimwit." One blast of power catapults him into the air, through the trees and out of sight.

I rip my arms free from the soldiers' grasp and snatch Licinia's dagger in one swift motion. I punch Licinia in the face. I hear a loud crunch as her orbital bone shatters. She collapses to the ground, blood gushing from her eye.

Soldiers dash towards me. I wave my arm. Blue lasers shoot from my palm like an automatic weapon. Soldiers scream as the lasers pierce them, smoke rising from their skin where they've been shot.

I run to Saria. One thought is all it takes to slash open the ropes that bind her. I take her hand.

Footsteps grow louder behind us. The ground shakes with the impact. I spin around, poised to fight. My shoulders fall in relief when I see the blue and gold uniforms. The Aurelian army is coming.

"Come," I say to Saria, pulling her down a trail. I run with her until I'm sure that there's no soldiers lurking nearby. "Climb up that tree." I whisper. "Hide until the battle is over."

"Come with me," Saria says.

"I'm going back to fight."

"Then I'll fight too," Saria says.

"You can't! You don't have any magic. You'll get killed. Listen to me and stay alive."

Saria wraps me in a fierce hug. "I'm scared this is the last time I'll ever see you." Tears glisten in her eyes. "I love you. We have so much lost time to make up for."

"I love you," I say. "I'll be okay. We'll spend so much time together that you'll be sick of me. I promise." It's a promise I'm not sure I can keep, but I'll say whatever it takes to keep her safe. I watch her climb up the tree, fading into the starless sky.

I take a deep breath and throw my shoulders back. I'm ready as I'll ever be. I bolt back to the battlefield.

I peek around a tree, watching the battle unfold. Hundreds of soldiers fight, using both magical and non-magical means. One soldier plunges a knife into the gut of an enemy. Magical beams strike another soldier, hurtling him to the ground.

I search for Damian, but I can't find him amongst all the movement and weapons. I pray that he isn't one of the lifeless bodies sprawled in the dirt.

In my periphery, a familiar light glows. The multi-color orb glimmers, ribbons of magic ascending into the sky, protected by a barricade of soldiers. When I focus on that area, I can hear King Keifer and Queen Taya, clear as day, as if they're right beside me. This blue magic stuff is pretty cool.

"We have to use it, Keifer. Our people are dying. Your son is out there fighting."

"He's a fool! The rest of the royals are safe behind castle walls."

"Keifer, one life is not more valuable than another. We cannot let our soldiers die. If Talon wins, he'll force his way into Aurelia. We won't have anyone left to fight."

"This is our most powerful weapon. We need to save it–"

"For a time like this!" Queen Taya says.

I hope that King Keifer makes the right call, but I don't have more time to eavesdrop.

I dart onto the battlefield, clambering over piles of bodies. As soldiers rush towards me, I lift my hands. Lightning-like bolts shoot from my fingertips, electrocuting several enemies. I kick another soldier in the nuts. The impact propels him ten feet into the air, where he lands tangled in a tree branch. As I get more familiar with my newfound power, I discover more and more abilities. When I flick my fingers, missile-like projectiles target my enemies and explode. One uppercut to an enemy's chin fractures his jawbone and every tooth in his mouth.

Beams of multi-color light soar through the air. A yellow beam wraps itself around an enemy's neck, strangling him to death. Once he lay on the ground, his breathing ceased, the yellow beam vanishes. An orange beam plunges into an enemy's mouth and bursts out of his abdomen, guts and blood splattering everywhere. When the soldier drops to the ground, the orange beam disintegrates.

King Keifer must've detonated the great ancestral scepter. Disembodied magic from hundreds of witches battles alongside us.

I don't slow down. I go harder. I kick and punch with a force that ruptures organs. I hurl mini-tornadoes that take my enemies to the ground. I launch grenade-like magic that blasts them apart. I will not stop until every enemy is taken down. I will not stop until I know that Damian is safe.

A headache hits me from out of nowhere, like a hammer to my skull. The searing pain tears down my body, penetrating every cell along its way. I crumple to my knees, struggling to stay upright. The world whirls around me. I topple over into a pool of bright red blood. As I fight to stay awake, I wonder if this is the end for me. I hope Damian knows that I love him. I hope Saria forgives me for breaking my promise. Darkness envelops me, and then I'm gone.

Chapter Twenty-Six

Saria

From my vantage point on top of the tree, it looks like a fireworks show. Purple, green, and orange explosions illuminate the night sky. Bangs, screams and pops echo on the wind. I cling to the branch, my heart rattling in my chest.

When the commotion dies down, I slide down the tree. I struggle to catch my breath: choking on the inky darkness, panting as my feet hit the ground.

I dart from tree to tree, taking cover and checking my surroundings before moving on. As I get closer to the battlefield, voices grow louder. When I reach the perimeter, bile rises in my throat. It's pure carnage: dead bodies, dismembered body parts, empty eyes. Is my sister amongst the blood and guts? Is she alive?

A soldier dressed in royal blue stands on top of a big rock. He clears his throat. "Attention! Attention!" His voice carries over the crowd. "King Keifer has an announcement."

The soldier steps down to make way for the king. Even on the battlefield, King Keifer wears an elaborate crown. "After a thorough search, my men report that the enemy is gone. All of Talon's men have either been killed or fled the scene. Aurelia has emerged victorious, but not without casualties.

"Our extraordinary medical team is making the rounds, working tirelessly to heal our wounded soldiers. Many civilians have arrived on the scene, searching for their loved ones. If you locate a loved one who needs medical attention, holler and a medic will get to you as soon as possible.

"While we may have won the battle, the war is just beginning. Talon Crowe and Licinia Wolfe, the masterminds behind this evil operation, have yet to be accounted for. We will not rest until they are found and put to death. They will pay for their crimes against Aurelia. Your loved ones will not die in vain. Aurelia will defeat Talon, Licinia, and anyone who aligns with their perverse ideology."

I step over dead bodies, my sneakers sloshing in blood, looking for my sister. It feels like an hour later when I spot her purple boots, splayed across the ground. Damian kneels over Zoeli's limp body, one hand on her wrist, the other on her heart. I run to her, my palms clammy and cold. "Is she okay?" I ask, dropping by her side.

"She's not injured," Damian says. "But she's suffering from severe MOSS." I'm familiar with the term. I remember the times Mom gave herself MOSS healing patients at the hospital. Back then, I was able to help, but now I'm useless. Maybe I should've let Zoeli transfer some power back to me. "I'm trying, but I'm not an advanced healer," Damian says. "I can heal minor cuts, but this is way beyond my abilities."

A woman approaches, her eyes bloodshot, her cheeks streaked with tears. The bottom of her blue cloak is soaked in blood. "How's she doing?"

"Not good, Mom," Damian says. "Zoeli didn't know how to prevent MOSS. She couldn't tell that she was using way too much magic at once. How could she? She wasn't allowed in our schools."

The queen shakes her head. "I'm sorry, Damian. You know I tried."

"Her pulse is getting weaker. If she doesn't get medical attention right away, she's not going to make it."

"Keifer!" The queen shouts. "Zoeli needs a medic–stat!"

The king saunters over, fully armored knights at his sides. "No one is available at the moment."

"There isn't time to waste. Pull a medic and send them over here."

"Dear, we must prioritize our own kind. I cannot skip over an Aurelian citizen for a nimwit. What king would allow that? Our people would be furious, and rightfully so. After every Aurelian is taken care of, she will be next. She's lucky I'm offering her medical care at all."

"She won't survive that long!" Damian shouts.

"So, it goes." The king shrugs and walks away.

"Saria! Zoeli!" Mom runs to me, her arms open wide. She squeezes me tight. "Thank God you're alive. I came as soon as I heard." Aunt Gwenna and Caliah follow behind. "What's wrong with her?" Mom asks, her gaze shifting to Zoeli.

"She has MOSS," Damian says. "You should've seen her in battle. She was incredible."

Mom places her fingers on Zoeli's neck, digging for a pulse. "She's so cold," Mom says, worry lines etched into her forehead.

"The medics won't help her because she's half-human," I say.

"I'll take care of her," Mom says, pressing her palms on Zoeli's chest.

Aunt Gwenna glances over her shoulder, like she's afraid she might be seen. "You're going to need help." Gwenna squats beside Zoeli. "Without the king's explicit permission, it's against the law to heal anyone with human blood," Gwenna whispers, catching my eye. "Tell me if you see him coming."

I stand in front of Aunt Gwenna, blocking her from the king's view. Damian stands beside me, watching Mom and Gwenna get to work. Caliah leans against him, resting her chest on his chest. "I was so worried about you," Caliah says. "Thank God you're okay."

That's when it hits me. Of course! He's the Prince of Aurelia. If I hadn't been tied to a tree and afraid for my life, I would've recognized him sooner. Caliah showed me his picture yesterday, her eyes lighting up, her cheeks flushed with excitement. Damian is engaged to marry Caliah.

Damian's eyes never leave Zoeli. My mom and my aunt work at a frantic pace, chanting softly as their hands glide over Zoeli's limp body. Damian's lower lip trembles, his face ghost-white. He may be engaged to marry Caliah, but he's in love with my sister. She probably loves him, too, which would explain why she was so upset after Caliah's announcement. My heart aches for my sister. If she survives, she might have to watch the person she loves marry someone else.

"She's warming up," Aunt Gwenna says.

"Her pulse is getting stronger," Mom says.

"He's coming!" I say. As King Keifer strides towards us, Aunt Gwenna stands and dusts off her knees.

"Ah, all three criminal Crowes are here. How nice of you to show up and save me the trouble of hunting you down." His lips curl up in a vicious smile. He gestures to his guards. "Arrest them. All three of them."

A guard grabs my wrists and pins them behind my back. I try to pull away, but he's much stronger than me. He twists my arm. As I howl in pain, handcuffs click into place.

"What's going on?" Mom asks as guards surround her. "I paid for my choices, and my daughters are innocent! You can't do this!" The guards close in around her, wrestling her arms behind her as she fights back.

"Alaina Crowe, you're charged with multiple counts of healing humans at Mountainside Hospital. In addition, you're charged with multiple counts of using sorcery in the presence of humans to a degree which jeopardizes our exposure."

"Saria Crowe, you're charged with disclosing confidential information to a human–"

"I did not!" I say.

"Did you or did you not tell Logan Archer about your magical abilities?"

"Wha–" My jaw drops. How does he know?

"Additionally, you're charged with multiple counts of utilizing magic for personal gain, bewitching humans, and using sorcery in the presence of humans to a degree which jeopardizes our exposure."

"It wasn't my fault!" I shout, but King Keifer has already moved on.

"Zoeli Crowe, you're charged with performing an unauthorized evulsion, bewitching humans and multiple counts of using sorcery in the presence of humans to a degree which jeopardizes our exposure." King Keifer sneers as Zoeli's limp body is lifted from the ground. Two guards hold her up by her armpits, her purple boots drudging through pools of blood. Her eyes open, then roll back into her head.

"Father, this isn't right," Damian says. "Zoeli fought for us. She's a hero. She deserves to be rewarded, not arrested. I demand that you drop all charges on Zoeli and her family, now!"

"Your demands mean nothing until you are king," King Keifer hisses. "Which may never happen at this rate."

Aunt Gwenna steps forward. "King Keifer, your majesty, with all due respect I believe that some of these charges fail to account for the whole picture."

Keifer waves her away. "They'll have their day in court." He turns to his guards. "Bring them to the dungeon."

Damian stands in front of Zoeli, his arms folded across his chest. "No," he says. "I won't allow it."

King Keifer moves so that his chest bumps into Damian's. "You don't have any say in the matter. Now, get out of the way before I have you arrested too." Nose-to-nose, the king and his son stare each other down. "Don't test me, Damian."

Reluctantly, Damian steps aside. The guards tighten their hands like a vise grip. I squirm, pain shooting down my arm. "Hold still, nimwit!" A guard smacks me across the face. My neck jerks back and my teeth clatter together. The guards chuckle.

I pray for a miracle as they drag me away.

Chapter Twenty-Seven

Zoeli

I shiver, my breath white in the darkness. The only light comes from the full moon, shining down from the tiny barred window.

How are you?
Cold and hungry.
I'll sneak down later. I'll bring snacks and turn on the heat.
Don't. It's not worth the risk. If you get arrested, how can you help get us out of here?
I'm doing everything I can to get your court date moved up. They scheduled it six months out, but I think I can pull some strings.

I lean against the stone wall, contemplating the horror of six months in this place. I stretch my legs out in front of me, accidentally nudging Saria with my toe. She shifts positions, rolling to her side, her hip on the hard floor.

"Dinner's served, nimwits." A guard slides a cardboard tray between the bars. It's the usual selection: two slices of stale bread and a hunk of moldy cheese. Tonight, they also included a half-rotten apple. It must be my lucky day.

The tray sits on the concrete floor, inches away from a grimy toilet. There's no privacy. When one of us is using the toilet, the other watches out for guards. At least we preserve a little dignity.

I pick up one slice of bread, and pass the other to Saria. Dirt is caked under my nails, but I'm too hungry to care. There's no sink, so we can't wash up. Every few days, a guard passes wet wipes and soapy sponges between the bars. Without a proper stream of water, it's impossible to get clean. Our cell stinks of grease and sweat.

Damian says there's a communal shower for the prisoners. Most are allowed supervised showers once per week, but I haven't been let out of this cell since I got here. The guards heard about my performance at the battle. They're afraid of me.

I've spent countless hours thrusting blue magic at the bars to no avail. The bars are made of katium, a rare metal that's impermeable to magic. Even if Mount Zamus erupted again, shooting the most potent of magic, the bars wouldn't bend or break. Katium cannot be destroyed by any means, magical or non.

Once, I hurled a blue laser between the bars, piercing a guard in his shoulder. As a punishment, they didn't feed us for two days. Saria writhed on the ground, moaning in pain, stomach acids gnawing her empty intestines.

I'll never make that mistake again. Watching my sister suffer was unbearable. In this godforsaken hellhole, the only blessing is that we're together.

"For so long, I thought I was crazy," Saria says. "I thought I was paranoid and losing my mind. I was always looking over my shoulder, convinced that someone was following me. After all this time, it turns out I was right. But who?"

We've been discussing this for days, trying to find the missing piece of the puzzle. "It must be the same person who left the evulsion instructions in my locker," I say.

"Maybe, but not necessarily." Saria finishes her last bite of bread, licking the crumbs off her bony fingers. Every day, she looks more skeletal. I'm not sure that we'll survive another six months in here.

"It could've been Aunt Gwenna," I say.

Saria shakes her head. "It doesn't add up. She risked her own ass to save your life. She wouldn't have leaked our secrets to Keifer."

"Don't underestimate her quest for power. She would've done anything to seal the deal of Caliah becoming queen. Maybe she saved me to assuage her guilty conscience."

"I guess, but I still think Mallory had something to do with this. She kept popping up everywhere: when Mom collapsed in the kitchen, at the softball game when someone was setting spells on me, in the woods before the tree fell on me, and in the parking lot when I was hanging out with Logan."

"Zoeli," A voice whispers in the darkness. I jump to my feet. Damian stands on the other side of the metal bars, his hand reaching through. "I brought you some muffins."

"I told you not to come! Where are the guards?" I whisper.

Damian grins. "They're taking a nap."

"Damian! You can't keep setting sleep spells on the guards. You're going to get caught." He's breaking one million laws to come down here, but I have to admit those muffins look amazing. I hand one to Saria, and then bite into another. Pure buttery goodness melts in my mouth. I actually moan. We're lucky if we're served more than a few slices of stale toast each day. "Thank you."

Through the bars, his fingers slip through mine. We put our foreheads against the metal, shifting until our noses find each other. His lips touch mine. I breathe out, and he breathes me in. "I love you, Zoeli. I'm going to get you out of here. One day, you're going to be my queen."

It's a pipe dream, but it sounds nice, so I nod. "I love you, Damian." Outside, wolves howl, their mournful call echoing inside the stone walls.

Epilogue

Dusk descends. Licinia's eyes pop open. She slides open the lid to her coffin and sits up. She climbs out, stretching her arm overhead. She doesn't have to look outside to know that it's a full moon. It's an itch inside her: the intense urge to shift.

As she ascends the basement stairs, the doorbell rings. A redhead waits on the front step. Licinia swings the door open. "Ah, my great-great-great-great niece Penelope. To what do I owe the honor?"

Penny slips inside and walks to the living room. She makes herself comfortable on the couch. Her crown-mark is visible in her strapless sundress, just above her collar-bone. "Talon's feeling much better. Every day he gets stronger. He'll be back to himself in no time."

"It's a shame he can't make a complete recovery during day sleep," Licinia says, touching her unmarred eye. "One of the many advantages to vampirism, I suppose."

"The Crowes are behind bars," Penny says, a grin spreading across her face.

"I heard," Licinia says. "Your little boyfriend came in handy for that."

"Ex-boyfriend," Penny clarifies. "He's furious at me. He was fine with taking down the Crowes, but I never told him about our plan to invade Aurelia. He was pretty upset about that." Penny shrugs. "I'll get him to forgive me if we find another use for him."

"Boys are so easy to manipulate," Licinia agrees.

"School's so much better now that Saria's gone. Pretending to be her friend was exhausting. It took every ounce of my self-control to stop myself from spitting in her face on a daily basis. A nimwit half-breed like her has no right to strut around like a celebrity."

"I guess that's why you gave Zoeli the evulsion instructions."

"I would've done the evulsion myself if we were compatible. I even ran a compatibility test, but no dice." Penny shrugs. "It was so sweet to watch her suffer after Zoeli got the job done."

"Yeah, but your little revenge plot could've killed me. I wasn't prepared for her to be so strong. She caught me off guard."

"You're fine now." Penny shrugs. "And we would've lost the battle regardless. It was the great ancestral scepter that defeated us, not Zoeli."

"I don't consider it a loss," Licinia says. "They drained their strongest weapon. That's a win in my book. Next time, we'll have no trouble getting into Aurelia."

A long howl cuts through the night.

"They're calling us," Licinia says.

"Let's go." There's a whirlwind of dust and smoke as skin transforms into fur, hands turn to paws, nails grow into claws. Two wolves soar through the open window and into the night. As they dart through the forest, creatures retreat, hiding beneath brush or inside hollow trees.

The wolves stand underneath the full moon, necks tilted up, releasing their guttural cry. They howl for the lives lost on their side, for pride in a victory of sorts, and as a promise of vengeance yet to come.

The End

Join Zoeli and Saria on their next adventure!
Book 2 of The Crowe Sisters Trilogy

MAGIC COMING UNDONE

is available NOW!

Jailed for little more than their identities, half-human, half-witch twins Zoeli and Saria endure torture and starvation in Nightingale Dungeon. As they struggle to escape, their biggest enemies, Uncle Talon and Licinia, hatch a plan to take over Aurelia, the supernatural realm, ensuring that the sisters will be imprisoned forever—or worse.

After one sister negotiates her release, she'll do anything to free her twin—including striking a deal with a handsome vampire. When she gets more than she bargained for, both her life and heart are at stake.

Their only hope for saving themselves and Aurelia is doing the impossible: reversing a decades old curse. Magic coming undone has a ripple effect: exposing betrayals and unraveling lies. The truths that are revealed destroy friendships and break hearts.

If they're strong enough, they'll pick up the pieces and put themselves back together. They'll even find that some things fall apart so better things can come together.

As Zoeli and Saria fight for one another and Aurelia, they discover that the greatest magic of all is the love between sisters. A true magic that can never come undone, as long as they make it through this battle alive.

Pick up your copy today! Available at Amazon, Kindle Unlimited, Barnes and Noble and many other online retailers worldwide.

https://www.amazon.com/dp/B0CXN18C8G

Want more YA fantasy romance from Faith Prince?

"A heart-warming story with incredible character development, Wild Souls isn't just about falling in love. It's about finding someone loves you for who you truly are, regardless of who the world perceives you to be. It's about overcoming your fears and facing your inner demons. Deep, meaningful, well-written, and at times laugh-out-loud funny, Wild Souls is a must-read for all ages."

Ethan sees right through skin and bone, his visions exposing the true nature of each person he meets. In his town, he's known as a freak and a liar. Completely ostracized, he keeps his head down and avoids people. After all, there's no point in uncovering the truth about people if no one believes you anyway. Everyone says he's insane. Yet, Jenna likes him.

Jenna has no idea that Ethan can see straight through to her soul. She doesn't know why he accuses upstanding citizens of heinous crimes—spurring hatred towards him throughout their small town. All Jenna knows is that he gets her offbeat humor and fascination with the paranormal. Spending time with Ethan is a welcome escape from wondering why her dad won't answer her calls…

Until Ethan's sixth-sense opens a gate to their souls—literally. As they face their inner-most demons, they could either fall apart or fall deeper in love than they ever imagined…

Pick up your copy today! Available at Amazon, Kindle Unlimited, Audible, Barnes and Noble and many other online retailers worldwide.

https://www.amazon.com/dp/B0B8NVNXZL

Faith Prince is the author of The Crowe Sisters Trilogy (Where Magic Begins, Magic Coming Undone, Twin Flames) and the stand-alone novel Wild Souls.

Besides writing, some of Faith's favorite things include: spending time with her family, reading, country music, cats, chocolate, coffee, traveling, and concerts, in that order.

Visit Faith's YouTube channel at
https://www.youtube.com/c/FaithPrinceAuthor

Signed paperbacks are available for purchase on my website.
www.faithprinceauthor.com

Follow me!

Instagram: https://www.instagram.com/faithprincewrites
Twitter: https://twitter.com/FaithPrinceAuth
TikTok: https://www.tiktok.com/@faithprinceauthor
Amazon: https://www.amazon.com/author/faithprince